THE STREET

Also by Michael Prescott

Manstopper
Kane
Shadow Dance
Shiver
Shudder
Shatter
Deadly Pursuit
Blind Pursuit
Mortal Pursuit
Comes the Dark
Stealing Faces
The Shadow Hunter
Last Breath
Next Victim
In Dark Places
Dangerous Games
Mortal Faults
Final Sins
Riptide
Grave of Angels
Cold Around the Heart
Chasing Omega
Blood in the Water
Bad to the Bone
Skin in the Game

THE STREET

MICHAEL PRESCOTT

The Street, by Michael Prescott
Copyright © 2017 by Douglas Borton
All rights reserved.

ISBN-13: 978-1543017083
ISBN-10: 1543017088

i

THIS IS THE story of a snake that swallowed itself, and of three summer days on the street where I grew up, three days that I lived twice.

My name—well, actually I'd prefer not to give my name. It's not important, and concealing my identity has become something of a habit with me. A bad habit, one of many. I could tell you to call me Ishmael, but I'm pretty sure it's been done.

People always say they don't know where to begin a story, but I know exactly where this one starts. It starts with the scudding of my shoes on pavement, the chuffs of my breath, the beat of my heart in my ears. And behind me, a block away but closing fast—other footsteps, as quick as my own.

It was midnight on an October night in the city—never mind which city; that's another thing I'll keep to myself. The streets were empty except for me and my pursuers, and quiet except for the sounds of the chase.

And a siren, rising in the background. Backup had been called in. The net was tightening.

I ran hard, splashing through puddles on the sidewalk. It had rained earlier in the evening. My coat flapped around me, slowing me down. I'd torn it while climbing the fence in the alley behind the bar. Snagged the hem on a crooked finger of wire and ripped it free as the cops closed in.

Was there a subway entrance around here? Probably, but I didn't know the neighborhood well enough to find it. This part of town was unfamiliar territory. I didn't know where I was going or what I was doing.

And I didn't know why I'd done ... what I'd done. I never knew. As always, the stupidly destructive part of me had leapt into action, bypassing thought and logic. Another of my episodes. Another night of skinned knuckles and bleeding hands.

The wind, kicking up, pelted me with a fine spray of droplets. A newspaper caught hold of my leg and humped it for half a block until another gust puffed it away.

I passed the ragged huddle of a street person in a pocket park. No one else was around. I had a fleeting impulse to conceal myself in the bushes. Stupid plan. I would inevitably be found, cowering like Saddam Hussein in his spider hole.

But I couldn't run much farther. Already I could taste the sour bite of nausea at the back of my throat, feel the burn of oxygen starvation in my lungs. At fifty-four, I was no marathoner. Only adrenaline had kept me going this long.

The footsteps behind me were more distinct. Looking back, I glimpsed a pair of sprinting silhouettes bearing down. One of them yelled an order to halt. Yeah, he actually said the word *halt*, like in a movie or something. His shout echoed off the brick faces of the crumbling brownstones that penned me in.

Ahead was a break in the buildings, a side street, coming up fast. It looked very much like my last chance. In the few seconds when I was out of sight, maybe I could duck into a doorway, steal a car, vanish down a storm drain. Desperate thoughts, but I was out of viable options, and I guess I was starting to panic.

Oh, hell, we're old friends by now, so I can be honest with you, right? There's no guessing about it. I was in full panic mode.

Back to prison. That was where they would send me. A long stretch this time. A decade or more. I would be an old man when I got out. Or I would die in there, die in a cage, like a lab rat or a zoo animal.

Sometimes, in nightmares, I would find myself screaming—just screaming for no reason—screaming until I woke up. I heard that scream now. Heard it in my head, rising in volume, growing in pressure, expanding to fill my skull.

As I turned the corner and plunged down the intersecting street, that scream was threatening to explode out of me in a rush of wailing chaos.

And then ... everything changed.

There's no good way to tell this part. I didn't understand it then, and I still don't. There was no transition, no blurred interim between one reality and another. It was as abrupt as changing a TV channel. A flick of God's finger on the remote, and I was in a different world.

Night was gone. The city was gone. The October chill—it was gone, too.

No brick walls around me. No sidewalk under my feet. I was still running, carried by momentum, but there was nothing to run from. No pursuing footsteps, no siren. No sounds at all but the thudding of my shoes on asphalt as I blinked in the soft pinkish light.

I stumbled to a stop in the middle of a tree-lined street, facing west. I knew it was west, because the sun was rising behind me, over the ocean. Oh, I couldn't actually see the ocean from where I stood; I was two blocks inland, and the terrain in this part of New Jersey was flat. Still, I could orient myself well enough. I'd grown up here, after all.

This was Miller Avenue, three blocks stretching from the boardwalk at Cove Beach to the brackish estuary of Trouble Pond, which would mirror the sunset at the end of this summer day.

And yeah, I knew it was summer. The warmth and humidity told me so. The fact that it had been autumn a few seconds earlier was admittedly a bit of a puzzler, but trivial in comparison to the question of how I'd traversed hundreds of miles and gone from midnight to dawn in an eyeblink.

The most sensible explanation was that I was dreaming. Maybe the chase through the city had been a dream also. Maybe none of it had happened—not the incident at the bar, not the other patrons yelling for a cop, not the police following me on foot when I'd charged down an alley too narrow for their squad car. My bloodied hands—maybe they'd been a dream also.

But when I looked down at my knuckles, they were still raw and red, a fragment of my old reality stubbornly persisting in this new one.

I didn't think I'd dreamed that part of it. But I might be dreaming now. Maybe I'd collapsed on the sidewalk, and my brain was manufacturing a vivid fantasy while I lay unconscious. Or I'd died of a heart attack. I might be in heaven ... or in hell, which would surely suit me better.

Not that I've ever been a believer. That harps and hellfire stuff leaves me cold. I've always figured that when you're dead, it's lights out, show over. And I've taken a good deal of comfort in that thought. The prospect of standing before the throne of an omnipotent judge doesn't exactly warm my heart. But of course nobody can be really sure. In that sleep of death, what dreams may come ... You know how it goes.

Truth was, neither of the above scenarios seemed very satisfying. I felt too real to be dreaming and too alive to be dead. Besides, I had no recollection of dying, and I didn't think that was a thing I would forget.

I felt for all the world as if I'd simply jogged onto Miller Avenue in the early morning light.

I looked around me, too bewildered to be afraid. Funny how the old neighborhood hadn't changed. It had been forty-four years since I'd lived here. My family had moved away in the fall of 1972. Yet everything was just as I remembered it. The same rows of little houses on small rectangular lots. The same willow trees in the yards and honey locust trees along the curb. Even the same cars parked in the driveways and on the street.

Not today's cars. Vintage models, none newer than the early '70s, yet all of them looking remarkably well preserved, as if they'd come off the assembly line just last week.

The cars were my first clue, but there were others. I heard no hum of air conditioners. I saw no satellite dishes on the roofs, no cable TV hookups. Garbage cans had been put out by the curb; I looked into one of them—paper and plastic and glass were freely mixed with scraps of leftovers. No recycling.

You could say a suspicion was forming in my mind, but that wouldn't be quite true. A person can't seriously suspect something that's impossible. And what I'd begun to imagine was obviously an impossibility according to all laws of science, not to mention the more compelling convictions of common sense.

Still, I couldn't deny the simple fact that everything I saw around me was consistent with my childhood memories. With life not in 2016, but four decades earlier.

I wondered if I'd finally snapped, finally lost it altogether, gone fully and irretrievably bonkers. It had always been a possibility. Maybe it had happened years ago. I could have spent most of my life in a mental hospital, lost in hallucinations and memories. Maybe nothing I knew was real, except this one part of it. This street, this summer day.

Kneeling, I touched the asphalt of the street—hard and pebbly, seamed with fine cracks. I reached over and felt blades of grass in the freshly mowed lawn of 110 Miller, where the two spinster sisters, Clara and Enid, had lived. The grass was dewy and cool. My fingertips came away wet. I pressed my hand into the soil and felt damp crumbs of earth.

And I was sure it was no dream or fantasy. Everything was too vivid, too richly textured.

When I looked up, I spotted a folded newspaper some distance away. It lay dead center in the middle of the lawn, having successfully missed the more obvious targets of the driveway and the porch. A paperboy must have tossed it there, making a predawn delivery, just as the local kid used to do when I was growing up. I even remembered that kid—the Epstein boy, Eddie or Ernest, something like that. I'd envied him because he made fourteen dollars a week riding around town on his Schwinn and throwing newspapers, not too accurately, at people's houses.

I crossed the lawn, feeling ridiculously conspicuous in my fur-lined coat, and scooped up the paper. It was damp with dew, but readable. The *Asbury Park Press*.

The front-page headline read *McGovern Scans List for Ticket*, with the subhead *Aides Say Kennedy Is Still Choice*. The story concerned the Tuesday session of the Democratic Party convention in Miami Beach. Other stories concerned IRA violence in Belfast and the resumption of peace talks negotiating an end to the Vietnam War.

The date on the masthead was Wednesday, July 12, 1972.

My stomach performed a little flip. It was one thing to suspect that I'd been transported back to the era of my childhood, and another to see confirmation in printer's ink on fresh newsprint.

Without thinking, I took the paper with me as I left the yard. If anyone had seen me, I might have gotten in trouble.

But you know what? It was beginning to look like I was in trouble already.

ii

I WALKED IN a kind of trance. The sun crawled an inch or two above the horizon. Already I was overheating in my coat. I don't think the summers were as warm in '72 as they are now—climate change and all—but we'd had occasional heat waves. And as I'd already observed, air conditioning had been a rarity. On hot nights you opened the windows and sweated it out.

Unsteadily I retraced my steps, going east, into the sun. I walked down the middle of the street because there were no sidewalks on Miller Avenue. Had I been a classic car enthusiast, I might have taken more of an interest in the automobiles parked along the curb. But I don't know jack about that stuff. I can't tell a V8 engine from a can of V8 juice.

Even so, I couldn't help noticing how clunky the cars looked, wide and boxy, all chrome and sharp angles. I peered into a window and saw a bare-bones interior—no video display, no GPS, no Bluetooth, no cruise control, not even a CD player or a tape deck. The car was unlocked, too. Anyone could just climb in and hot-wire it. Evidently no one would.

Overhead, a flock of seagulls flapped past, returning to the beach after a night spent inland. Had they been a choir of angels or a squadron of flying monkeys, they wouldn't have rocked my world. I was beyond the very possibility of surprise.

By now I was approaching the intersection of Miller and First Avenue, just one block from the boardwalk. A random corner, much like the corner I'd turned in the city.

But for me it was Ground Zero, my point of entry to this waking dream.

If there was some sort of portal at that spot, a wormhole or a teleporter or some damn thing—a direct connection between different points in space and time—then possibly I could use it as an exit as well as an entrance. The idea seemed far-fetched, but so did my entire situation.

Right now I wanted nothing more than to get back to where I'd been, even if it meant resuming the chase, even if it meant capture and prison. I wanted things to make sense again. I wanted my old life back, the life I knew, with rules I understood. Strange, isn't it, how you'd give anything to get out of the mess you've made of your life, and as soon as you're home free, all you want is what you've lost?

Listen to me. Philosophizing.

Anyway, I was all gung-ho to test my theory. But as I drew closer to the corner, inexplicably my feet began to drag. The soles of my shoes scuffed the asphalt. I seemed to be slogging through deep mud, quicksand. The street grabbed hold of my feet with increasing tenacity. It became a struggle merely to raise a leg and take a step.

A few feet from the corner, I stopped. I could go no farther.

As a kid, I'd had a pair of magnets. When I turned them so the positive poles were facing each other, the repulsive force between those poles made it impossible to bring them together. An invisible field held them immovably apart.

Ground Zero was repelling me as surely as those magnets had repelled each other.

So apparently there was no going back. I was stuck here, wherever and whenever *here* might be.

It wasn't necessarily the worst outcome. If this was hell or purgatory, it could have been a lot more unpleasant. If it was some glitch in the fabric of space-time, at least it had landed me in a safe, familiar spot, as opposed to, say, the arena of the Colosseum or a stateroom on the *Titanic*.

What can I say? I'm a glass-half-full kind of guy.

I plopped myself down on the curb and thought things over. If I was here for the duration, however long the duration might be, I needed a plan of action. Right now I stood out like Kim Kardashian at a Mensa meeting. My outfit was all wrong. I was dressed for autumn—leather coat, corduroy shirt—in clothes that were current in 2016. From what I remembered of 1972, the fashions had been decidedly different.

Before long, the residents of Miller Avenue would begin to stir. Assuming, of course, that there were other people here, and that this wasn't a movie-studio street of cunning façades. I didn't want to see any people right away. More to the point, I didn't want them to see me.

What I needed was to lie low for a while and also find a way to camouflage myself. I was pretty sure the answer to both problems lay at the opposite end of the street, by Trouble Pond.

I shed my coat, draped it over my arm, and set off in that direction. As I walked, I tried estimating the length of the block. Nine houses on each side of the street. Each lot fifty feet wide. Unless my math skills had seriously deteriorated since first grade, the total was four hundred fifty feet. The street ended in a cul-de-sac at the pond. I wasn't going farther west unless I swam for it, and I had no idea how far I could progress to the north or south.

I might be stuck on this one patch of real estate, smaller than two football fields. And in New Jersey, to boot.

Halfway down the block, I came face to face with a little white bungalow at 114 Miller, the house where I'd grown up. And the thought crept up on me that in an upstairs room of that house, in a twin bed by a window with a view of the willow tree in the backyard, lay a ten-year-old boy who was me. If that was even possible. I mean, they say two objects can't occupy the same space at the same time, right? Well, then, could two me's exist side by side in the same reality? It seemed like a question worth tweeting to Neil Degrasse Tyson, but Twitter hadn't been invented yet.

I pondered what would happen if I were to encounter my 1972 doppelgänger. Would he know me? Or would I be just some generic old guy to him? Could he read my mind, or could I read his? Or would the universe implode, as in some meeting of matter and antimatter?

The whole thing was just too weird. It was starting to seriously freak me out.

I reached the pond, which was really more of a lake, given its size and depth. It was rumored that in earlier centuries, wayward ships had run aground there, thus explaining the word *trouble* in its name.

On impulse I turned north, cutting across the O'Keefes' side yard. Mr. and Mrs. O'Keefe—I remembered them—and their daughter Lily, who'd been older than me. And a sheepdog named, um, Tiger. Right, like the dog on *The Brady Bunch*. It was all coming back, a floodtide of memories.

The property line at the rear of the O'Keefes' yard was as far as I got. I'd come up against another invisible barrier.

I retraced my steps. South of Miller Avenue, a dense stand of woods skirted the pond. I plunged into it, following a trail I'd taken as a kid when I'd come here to play with my G.I. Joes. That was back when they still made good G.I. Joes, bigger and more realistically articulated than the crappy ones from 2016. I would arrange them in the tall grasses and on the rocks, playing at war with my friends. Meanwhile, real-life G.I. Joes were fighting and dying in rice paddies half a world away, but somehow we never thought about that.

The trail took me to a narrow channel linking Trouble

Pond to the sea. By then I was starting to feel a mite claustrophobic, and I believe I would have been willing to wade into the creek in an effort to cross it, but I didn't have that option. I encountered yet another force field, or whatever it was, at the water's edge. I stood there, helpless. Houses lined the opposite bank, close enough to hit with a well-aimed slingshot, but for me they were as distant as villas in the south of France.

So that was it: the exact dimensions of my hamster cage. One small-town street, eighteen houses on postage-stamp lots, and a tangle of overgrown vegetation. If I was going to spend eternity here, it would be a long stay.

In the city I'd worried about a police siren and a tightening net. Well, the net had been well and truly tightened now.

I doubled back through the woods. My immediate objective was the gray-shingled house that butted up against these woods at the southwest corner of Miller Avenue. Mr. and Mrs. Stevenson's house.

I hadn't thought of them in forty-four years, and an hour ago I might not have remembered their last name. Now I recalled distinctly that the Stevensons, who used their home at 119 Miller as a vacation retreat, had been away all summer—off in Europe or something. If this reality was, in fact, the summer of 1972, or even a close simulation, then the Stevenson place ought to be unoccupied.

I only had to get inside. It meant entering uninvited, but what the hell. I'd entered this entire reality uninvited, hadn't I?

By now I'd left the trail and was blundering through a green wall of bulrushes and cattails. It occurred to me that the woods must be crawling with ticks in summer. I worried briefly about Lyme disease, before remembering that there was no Lyme disease in 1972.

The sun was higher in the sky, a smear of yellow glare.

Everything seemed perplexingly real, though my rational mind told me it couldn't be. I'd gone over the rainbow, through the looking glass, into the Twilight Zone. I kept waiting for Rod Serling to show up, cigarette in hand, and explain what was going on. There had to be a neat little moral in this story somewhere.

The Stevensons' backyard was conveniently unfenced. Their back door was locked, but there was no indication of an alarm system—not that I'd expected one in this neighborhood in 1972. Parts of America might be burning in urban riots, even some nearby towns, but violence had never touched this street.

Except... that wasn't true, was it? Something *had* happened here, in the summer of this year. In this very month, I thought. Something my parents never spoke of in later years. Something that had left me traumatized and ... *changed*. It was why we'd moved away in the fall. I knew that much, but I'd never known any details. The episode had been wiped from memory.

Even now, I had no distinct recollection of it. Yet I'd remembered the Stevensons and their European vacation, the O'Keefes and their dog. If I could retrieve those bits of trivia, why could I recall nothing about an event that had to be a million times more important?

I tabled the question. Now was not the time to play *I Love a Mystery*. I had enough of a mystery on my hands as it was.

A fist-size rock took care of a window at the rear the house. The glass didn't make much noise when it shattered, and I doubted the neighbors had heard.

As I brushed the clinging shards out of the frame, it occurred to me that I just taken a possibly momentous step. I had altered my environment. A pane of glass that had been intact was now in pieces. Wasn't there a Ray Bradbury story about a time traveler who steps on a bug and rewrites the future? If this really was the past, I might have just changed the course of history. Maybe 9/11 wouldn't happen now, or *Seinfeld* wouldn't make it past the first six episodes, or McDonald's would never introduce the McRib sandwich—all because I'd smashed the Stevensons' rear window.

Hey, *que sera, sera*. I needed shelter. The future would have to take care of itself.

I climbed through the window and explored my new digs. I'd forgotten how small the houses were in this era. Not just the total floor space, but the individual rooms. Walls were everywhere. Space that could have been relatively large and open was broken up into cubbyholes—a pocket-sized dining room, an even smaller kitchen, bathrooms so tiny you could hardly turn around.

The decor was straight out of *The Dick Van Dyke Show*. You remember the brick wall in Rob and Laura's living room? Its twin was here, along with shag carpet in garish orange and red shades, and kitchen appliances done up in earth tones.

The Stevensons had only one TV, a nineteen-inch General Electric resting on a metal cart in a wood-paneled ground-floor retreat that they probably called a rec room. That's what we'd called an almost identical room in our place. The TV had two large dials on the front and a rabbit-ears antenna sticking out of the top. I turned it on and rotated the dial, flipping through the channels—all four of them. CBS, NBC, a local station out of New York, and PBS. Apparently ABC's signal didn't reach the boonies yet. The picture was in color, but reception was poor—a succession of bleary, ghosted images striped with horizontal lines of interference. Not everything about 2016 was great, but the entertainment technology had 1972 beat by a mile.

There was little on the tube—PBS was still broadcasting a test pattern, and the other three stations showed cartoons. I switched it off and went upstairs to the top floor, where I found the master bedroom. Mr. and Mrs. Stevenson slept in twin beds. Again, just like Rob and Laura.

I used the bathroom, taking a whiz. It turns out even time travelers have to pee.

Afterward, I checked myself out in the mirror—not out of vanity, mind you, but just to make sure I was really there. This is the part where I ought to give you my description. You know, add detail and texture to the story. Screw it. You don't need to know what I look like. Make up your own picture. If you're anything like me, it's what you'll do anyway.

I ran water in the sink and washed the dried blood off my knuckles. The blood bothered me, because there was so much, and most of it was hers.

I hadn't meant to go all batshit on the woman. It was the way she'd looked at me. Something in her frightened, staring eyes, though I'd done nothing to alarm her.

You see, I have what you might call anger management issues. A problem with impulse control. It's just a little too easy to press my buttons. Most times, I don't even know what triggered me. I only know that I see red—literally— a burst of red, dazzling like fireworks.

I couldn't even blame this one on alcohol, though it had happened in a bar. I'd stopped in there, a place I'd never been before, a sad little dive, after wandering for hours down random city streets. I didn't know the neighborhood, and I was feeling lost in more ways than one. One drink couldn't hurt, I thought.

In fact, I'd had just one drink, though I would've had another, if I'd been given the chance. As it happened, I used the men's room after my first round, and as I stepped back into the hall, I bumped into a woman coming the other way, and she turned and looked at me. Just looked.

That was all it took. I saw her stupid face, her dazed cow eyes, and everything went red and I was beating her head against the wall, and people at the other end of the hall were shouting. I left her there, a sprawled mess, but alive—probably alive—and escaped through a rear exit, sure I could get away. By sheer bad luck, a squad car was cruising the neighborhood, near enough that the patrolmen caught sight of me. Hence, the chase.

The cops hadn't seen me up close, the neighborhood was one where nobody knew me, and I doubted that anyone in the bar could provide a decent description. I'd paid cash for my drink—no credit card on file. My prints weren't even on the glass; I'd watched the bartender wipe it clean. Having magically made my getaway, I saw no likelihood that the authorities would ever track me down.

Of course, the issue of my legal culpability was moot for the time being. As long as I was a castaway in 1972, the only way the police from 2016 were going to get their hands on me was if one of them was Jean-Claude Van Damme.

Get it? *Timecop* reference? Oh, come on. This whole thing will go a lot easier if you work with me.

Okay, I know what you're thinking. You've got me pegged as an unreliable narrator. You think I couldn't possibly have been this cool about my situation. You think I must have been curled up in a fetal ball, whimpering, with my thumb in my mouth. I wasn't making dumb movie jokes and calmly inspecting the premises; I was having a nervous breakdown. Right?

I hear you. In retrospect I'm mildly astonished at my blasé attitude. But you know what? Denial ain't just a river. At some level I still didn't think any of this was actually happening. As a result, I was operating on reflex, just carrying on, the way you do in a dream when nothing makes sense but you keep going anyway.

Or maybe I was just too dumb and unimaginative to be really afraid.

Anyhow, I checked out the rest of the house, experiencing

a recurrent feeling of déjà vu because it was so much like the one where I'd grown up. All the homes on this block were cast from the same mold, put up at the same time by the same developer. In the postwar era, conformity was a feature, not a bug.

By then, I was tired. It wasn't shock—well, it wasn't *just* shock. It was also plain exhaustion. Call it metaphysical jet lag. For my confused body, the time was around one AM, and the rising sun did nothing to persuade it otherwise. I wandered into the living room and sat in an armchair, well away from any windows so as not to be seen from outside, and flipped through the newspaper I'd brought with me, only half seeing the columns of text.

Boris Spassky was favored over Bobby Fischer in a world chess championship. Female pilots were competing in a cross-country airplane race called, condescendingly enough, the Powder Puff Derby. Eight divorces had been granted in the county, the names of the couples listed like a roll call of shame. The forecast called for increasing cloudiness with scattered rain overnight and tomorrow.

After a while the paper must have slipped from my fingers and drifted to the floor. That was where I found it when I woke up nine hours later.

A long sleep, mercifully dreamless. Yet to my disappointment, I was still in the Stevensons' house, hot and stuffy with the windows closed. Still a fish out of water, a man out of time.

I wondered if nine hours had passed in 2016. If so, the police would have long since given up their pursuit. No one else would miss me. My boss would wonder what had become of me, but he wouldn't really care. Other than that, there was nobody. No wife or significant other, no kids, no dog, not even a guppy in a fishbowl. No commitments. I wasn't the type to get close to anyone. For a man like me, there were too many ways it could go wrong.

I picked up the paper, which had fallen open to a

random page. One story caught my eye—a series of break-ins here in town. Houses burglarized in the middle of the day, when no one was home. Items had been stolen, though no details were provided. There was no suspect, and the break-ins seemed to be progressing southward, closer to this end of town. This street.

The tingle at the back of my neck was the short hairs prickling—one of the few times in my life when they'd actually done that. A memory stirred. No, not quite a memory. An impression, a hint. Something about a break-in, an intruder.

And screaming. Screaming ...

I closed my eyes, and I could hear that scream now.

iii

BY THE TIME I roused myself, it was after four o'clock in the afternoon. I was hungry, but still too frazzled to think about cooking anything. I found a box of Cap'n Crunch and ate handfuls of the sugary stuff straight out of the box. No milk in the fridge.

Then I decided to test the barrier again. Why not? Maybe the rules had changed. And I couldn't hide in this house forever.

First, though, I took a shower—a good one; no low-flow shower heads in this era. No low-flow toilets, either—just listen to that flush! A man could drop a serious load in 1972.

In the bedroom closet and a tall dresser next to it, I found the husband's things. He seemed to be about my size—close enough, anyway, that I could wear his stuff without looking like a fool. Well, let me rephrase that. These were clothes from 1972. You remember the styles from that era, don't you? Anyone wearing those outfits couldn't help but look like a fool. But that was okay. I only needed to blend in. When in Rome, do as the Romans do. Had I been teleported to Julius Caesar's day, I would be getting fitted for a toga by now.

I stripped off my shirt and pants, then tarted myself up in hideous striped trousers and a canary yellow shirt. They were the least flamboyant items I could find. I wasn't trying to call attention to myself, believe me.

I left my shoes on, after polishing them with a hand towel to remove rain spatter from the city and soil from the woods. I didn't think I could squeeze my feet into Mr. Stevenson's footwear, and I figured one pair of shoes looks pretty much like another. An expert might have detected telltale signs of modernity in my Bruno Maglis, but I wasn't planning to let anyone get that close a look.

I did switch out my watch. The one I'd been wearing was digital, a Fossil with all the bells and whistles. I substituted a no-nonsense Timex I had to wind by hand. I left my cell phone in a drawer. First time I'd been without it in years. In this world, where there were no cell towers and no Wi-Fi hotspots, it was essentially a paperweight.

When I transferred my wallet to my borrowed pants, I realized I had a new problem. The cash inside was the twenty-first century version, with holograms and special tints and outsized presidential faces. It would look like Monopoly money in 1972. My credit cards were obviously useless; those accounts hadn't even been set up yet, the account owner being ten years old in this reality. Driver's license, bank card, even a coupon for Whole Foods that I'd stuck in there—all of it was as out of place as a leisure suit in 2016.

I was going to find it difficult to function in this time period without money or ID. Then again, if I couldn't leave this street, it might not matter. Shopping wasn't going to be a problem if I was unable to get to any stores.

Sometime after four thirty, I finally ventured out via the side door, locking it behind me—I'd found a spare key in a drawer—and made my way through the woods to the bank of Trouble Pond. A few people were down on the rocks some distance away, setting crab traps in defiance of posted warnings. Pond rats, we used to call them—scruffy old guys, the only ones willing to eat shellfish drawn from the polluted estuary, which even in '72 was basically eight acres of fecal matter.

It occurred to me that if I was stuck here indefinitely, the Stevensons' food supply was sure to run out. Since I had no spendable money and no access to stores, I'd be in quite a pickle. Not to mention that the Stevensons would eventually drop in for a visit and find me there, like Goldilocks squatting in the Three Bears' cottage. I didn't anticipate a happy ending to that fairy tale.

Well, maybe I would end up as a pond rat myself, and homeless to boot, camping out in the woods and living off crabs and other unsavory marine delicacies fished out of Trouble Pond. For how long? Would I live out my allotted lifespan on this street? If I survived another thirty years, I'd make it to 2002. George W. Bush would be president. It didn't seem like something to look forward to.

There was a lot to worry about, but for the moment I decided my best course was not to think about any of it. I would only make myself crazy, assuming I wasn't crazy already.

Though I felt absurdly conspicuous in my new duds, no one paid me any attention as I strolled east along the street. Thanks to the overflow from beach parking, more cars than before lined the curb. Two mini-skirted girls with bare midriffs were unlocking a sporty little Datsun. A souped-up Plymouth Barracuda rolled past, crowded with teenage boys who let loose a chorus of lusty wolf whistles. The girls took no offense. They sashayed flirtatiously.

What's that quotation? The past is another country; they do things differently there.

Once more I passed 114 Miller, the home of my childhood. Across the street, a couple of doors down, was Mrs. McCall's house. She was a young widow or a divorcee—I'd never been quite sure which—who sometimes babysat for me. I'd had a bit of a crush on her, though I don't think I ever knew her first name. She would have been, what, about thirty-five in 1972? I hoped to get a glimpse of her, just for old times' sake.

"God *damn* it."

I glanced to my left and saw a woman kneeling by the flower garden at 110 Miller, sucking her finger. She looked at me and smiled.

"Pardon my language," she said. "I pricked myself on a thorn."

I didn't think someone from 2016 would consider her language to be worth apologizing for. I'd forgotten what a PG world this was.

Not wishing to appear suspiciously standoffish, I approached her. The house, two doors down from where I lived as a boy, was the one owned by the two sisters, Clara and Enid. I remembered them as superannuated crones, plausible stand-ins for the witches in *Macbeth*, and I was somewhat taken aback to realize that this one was probably about the same age I was now.

"Clara Ewing," she said, extending her hand and then quickly retracting it as she remembered her bloody fingertip.

I almost gave my real name, but no, that wouldn't do at all. Had I been more clever, I would have used a famous name from my own era, the way Michael J. Fox called himself Clint Eastwood in one of the *Back to the Future* movies. I could have been Brad Pitt or Daniel Craig. But I wasn't that quick on my feet.

"John Walker," I said, realizing only after the words were out that I was thinking of my favorite brand of scotch.

"Live around here, Mr. Walker?"

Mr. Walker, she'd called me. Not John. 1972 was a more formal time.

Improvising again, I said I was staying with friends the next town over. Before she could press for details, I switched the subject to flowers. I know nothing about gardening, but I conveyed the impression that I was a bona fide connoisseur. Clara immediately began filling me in on all aspects of the cultivation of roses. I feigned interest, wondering when I could make a polite exit.

"Clara, who are you talking—oh."

A second middle-aged woman had materialized on the

porch. Enid, obviously.

Introductions were made. This time I didn't hesitate before giving my fake name. In short order, Enid had invited me up to the porch for lemonade, and I was sitting on a creaky swing with a frosted glass in my hands while the two sisters chatted.

They seemed glad for the company. Lonely, I thought. Truthfully, I didn't think most of their neighbors, my parents included, had ever had much to do with them. Everyone except Mrs. McCall had treated them with cordial reserve. As a kid, I hadn't really noticed. Hadn't thought about them at all, except at Halloween, when they always gave out the best candy.

For sisters, they didn't look much alike. Even their way of speaking was subtly different. Clara had the ghost of a southern dialect, while Enid sounded more New England. They bickered like an old married couple, with the same impatience, the same resigned affection.

Okay, I'm a little slow on the uptake. It took me a good fifteen minutes to figure out they weren't sisters. They were two women who lived together, at a time when such things just weren't done—or more accurately, when they were done but not spoken of.

The realization intrigued me. I felt myself warming to them. They were outcasts, like myself—two people who didn't quite belong here, who could never really fit in. They felt modern somehow, a part of the future that had sneaked into the past, as I had. They made me feel less alone.

I was on my second cup of lemonade, fresh squeezed from lemons that grew in their backyard, when a kid's bike flashed past, turning into the driveway at 114 Miller.

There was only one kid who lived there in 1972, and I was looking at him, and he was me.

I saw my ten-year-old alter ego ditch his bike on the lawn and run to the back of the house. I tried not to stare. To say it was a weird feeling would be an understatement.

From a distance he could have been any kid, and if he hadn't stopped at the house I might not even have recognized him. But knowing who he was, watching him from a hundred feet away ... well, I wasn't sure just what I felt.

Sadness, perhaps. Yes, sadness, because I knew the future waiting for that boy, the stupid mess he would make of his life. All of that was as yet unwritten—or maybe it had been written. I'd lived it, hadn't I?

"Mr. Tibbs!"

That was Clara, scolding an overfed Siamese cat who retreated into the house.

Seeing that cat gave me a guilty start. I looked hastily away.

"He's not supposed to be outside," Clara explained. "He's an indoor cat."

"Sometimes he noses open the screen door," Enid added. "He's such a mischievous creature. We have to keep an eye on him every minute."

But I knew they wouldn't keep a close enough watch on Mr. Tibbs.

Some unconscious association of ideas led me to raise the subject of the local burglaries. I asked if they'd hit this neighborhood.

"Not yet." Enid's expression was grim.

"They say he steals ladies' things," Clara said. "You know. Their *things*."

Euphemisms were still pretty big in '72. I took it Clara meant underwear.

"And we all know who's doing it," Enid said.

"Enid!"

"Well, it's true."

"We don't know. We only *think*. It's gossip and speculation."

"Grounded in fact."

I asked what they were talking about.

"Mr. Wilson," Clara said, as if everyone knew.

They both told the story, freely interrupting each other and finishing each other's thoughts. It seemed a certain

Mr. Wilson had commenced renting 113 Miller at the start of the summer. This Mr. Wilson was nothing like the lovably grumpy old fart of *Dennis the Menace* fame. He was thin and spare, bespectacled and bald, and very quiet, unwilling to exchange more than two words with anyone. He seemed especially tongue-tied around women. He could never look them in the eye. And he watched people. He had been seen peering out through his curtains—like Mrs. Kravitz on *Bewitched*, Enid said—studying folks as they walked past, and even watching children at play.

That last part triggered a recollection. I had forgotten all about Mr. Wilson, but now I remembered the face in the window, the unnerving way he'd stared at us kids as we performed wheelies on our bikes. My parents had cautioned me to steer clear of him. They hadn't mentioned anything about burglaries, and certainly not women's undergarments, and I doubt I'd ever known about any of that. But they'd been worried by Mr. Wilson. It appeared they hadn't been alone.

To the sisters, I allowed that Mr. Wilson sounded like a peculiar fellow, all right, but was that any reason to suspect him of housebreaking?

"You're just like the police," Enid said impatiently. "They say they can't arrest somebody, or even search his house, without more to go on. But I *know* it's him. The burglaries keep getting closer and closer. He's gaining confidence, working closer to home. That's why I say he'll be doing it here before long."

"Well, he'd better not try pawing through my sock drawer," Clara said. Another euphemism. "If I should catch him, I'd give him what-for. Like that man at the Yankees game—remember, Enid?"

The conversation shifted to a brute who'd spilled beer on Clara in a baseball stadium, and his ensuing comeuppance. I drifted away again. I was thinking of Mr. Wilson.

Suppose Enid was right about him. Suppose he really

was breaking into houses and venturing progressively nearer to his home turf. They were the only local crimes I knew about. And they could tie in—maybe—with the trauma I'd suffered, or was about to suffer, this summer. If he'd broken into our house while I was home ...

A trespasser. An intruder.

Once again, those short hairs at the back of my neck stood at attention.

I was still pursuing this line of thought when a VW Beetle festooned with flower decals pulled into the driveway across the street. Mrs. McCall got out, and the sisters hailed her.

She was their only friend in the neighborhood, the one person cool enough to hang with them. She crossed the street and joined us on the porch, and we talked about McGovern and who his running mate would be and whether he had a chance against Nixon, who even then had earned the sobriquet Tricky Dick.

Her first name, it turned out, was Liz. She had vibrant red hair, piled high, and big sunglasses, tinted red, and long legs, made longer by absurdly high platform shoes. She wore a monochrome neon-green pantsuit, an undeniable fashion faux pas by my standards, but I couldn't hold it against her. As Grampa Simpson would say, that was the style at the time.

I liked her. I always had. As a kid, I'd looked forward to the nights when she would babysit. I hadn't even minded the troubling implications of the word *baby* in her job description.

Her actual job, it developed, was in the nearest large town—something to do with marketing and publicity. She wore no wedding ring and mentioned no boyfriend. It occurred to me that she might be gay, like Clara and Enid, but I doubted it. I didn't get that vibe.

Not that it mattered. I wasn't going to be starting any relationships here.

By now all three women had lit up. Cigarette smoke wafted through the porch. Even in '72, people had known smoking wasn't good for them, but most of them had done it anyway.

There was talk of recent disturbances in Long Branch, which led Clara to narrate one of her favorite stories—a thrilling episode two years ago in which she was caught up in the Asbury Park riots. The underprivileged, as she quaintly termed them, had been looting and burning, and she'd found herself trapped on Springwood Avenue in her Chevy Vega. The way she told it, she'd barely gotten out.

I remarked that it sounded like a near-death experience. Nobody knew what I was talking about. The term hadn't been coined yet.

The three ladies speculated glibly on how long it would take the burned-out resort town to rebuild. Both thought it might be as long as another five years. I could have told them that forty-four years would pass, and the job still wouldn't be finished. But they would never have believed me. People were more optimistic in this era. They had a can-do attitude born of naïveté. You could cure poverty by declaring war on it. You could end war by giving peace a chance. The solutions to all problems were as simple as John Lennon's lyrics to "Imagine." My world—your world, too—is different. In our world, John Lennon had been gunned down in the street.

The sisters mentioned that they were going to the movies on Friday night. They had yet to decide between *Cabaret,* Clara's choice, and *Frenzy,* Enid's vote. They were kind enough to invite Liz and me along. Yes, both of us. I wondered if they were trying to play matchmaker.

Naturally I begged off, knowing that anything outside this block was off-limits to me. Liz couldn't go, either; she was babysitting that night. Babysitting for me, as insane as that sounds.

I asked if she babysat often.

"Only for this one boy. I like him. He's very sweet. But sometimes I worry."

"About what?"

"He's so quiet and introspective. I think he's very sensitive."

"Is that bad?"

She bit her lip. "The world can be hard on the sensitive ones. They're so easily bruised. And sometimes the bruises never fade."

I couldn't argue with that.

Shortly afterward, Liz announced she was going home to make dinner. I took it as my cue to leave also. It was past six o'clock by then, and though the summer day was long, an overcast sky had brought on a premature twilight. In the humid stillness I walked with her to her front door. We chatted about this and that.

She was different from twenty-first century women. Or maybe it would be more correct to say that femininity itself was different in this decade. She was in good shape, but without the toned, sculpted physique favored by the women of my time. She had more curves, more of a bounce in her step. When she talked, she ducked her head charmingly, and she had this way of biting her lip. She wasn't girlish or childlike, nothing like that, but she wasn't competing for alpha status. Call me a knuckle-dragging sexist troglodyte, but I liked it.

"You know," she said as we were parting, "you remind me of someone. I can't quite put my finger on it."

"You think we've met before?" I asked.

"No. I'm sure we haven't." Another shy bob of her head, her eyes looking up at me from behind long lashes. "I'd remember."

I got out of there with a mumbled good-night. I might not be the best at reading signals, but what I'd seen in her face and heard in her voice was an unmistakable come-on.

That could be bad. There was danger in entering a relationship. It could lead to trouble.

And on Miller Avenue, there would be no escape.

Unless the force field was down. Maybe now it was. Maybe I could pass through the gateway, to be teleported back to the America of Donald Trump and self-driving cars and endless *Spider-Man* reboots.

I headed straight for Ground Zero, determined to get through.

But I couldn't, of course. The barrier was still in place, as impregnable as ever. This time I forced myself to go a step or two farther, fighting the resistance that increased exponentially with every inch of progress. Finally, when I was still a good two yards from the intersection, I quit. I literally could not move forward. I would be stuck like a fly in amber if I tried. Retreat was my only option.

Defeated, I went home. Well, I went to the Stevensons' home. You know what I mean.

By this time I was famished, so I took a closer look at the kitchen. In the pantry I found cans of pork and beans, corned beef hash, and Manwich sloppy-joe sauce. None of the labels provided nutritional information. It would be like chowing down on mystery meat.

The freezer showed greater promise. It was stocked with TV dinners. I settled on Swanson fried chicken, whipped potatoes, vegetables, and fruit slices, all in separate compartments in an aluminum tray.

Heating it in the oven only made the house hotter, but I was still reluctant to open any windows and possibly advertise the fact that it was occupied. I did risk turning on a single light after carefully drawing the curtains. I hoped the neighbors weren't overly inquisitive. If the police showed up, I'd have a hard time convincing them that I was a character out of an H.G. Wells story.

To be honest, I wasn't sure I was Wells' time traveler, anyway. Right now, burrowed in my shadowed lair, I bore a closer resemblance to one of his Morlocks. And the townsfolk outside were the Eloi—cheerful innocents who dressed like children, enjoying an endless summer.

I dined in the rec room, in front of the TV on its conveniently movable cart. Convention coverage had started. I watched Walter Cronkite on CBS. The delegates were in the process of nominating George McGovern to be the next president of the United States. Yeah, good luck with that.

It occurred to me that of all the time periods to which I could have been exiled, I'd ended up in the one where Richard Nixon was president. I can't say it made me feel any better about my situation.

And yet I was beginning to think my presence here was not accidental. I was beginning to suspect a larger purpose. It scared me, because it offered something new to me, something I hadn't known in a long time.

It offered hope.

iv

THE CONVENTION WAS not well organized. Nothing went off on schedule, and nobody seemed to be in charge. McGovern's support seemed to consist mostly of angry hippies and befuddled union chiefs. I was beginning to remember why Nixon had cruised to reelection despite being not only Tricky Dick, but also a regular dick.

I couldn't channel surf because there was no remote control, which meant I would have to get up and change the channels by hand—you know, like an animal. Besides, there weren't enough channels to surf, and the few that were available were stuck on the convention. No wonder there was so much middle-class conformity in this era. Everybody watched the same shit. How much of a rebel could you be when your only sources of information were Walter Cronkite paraphrasing the *New York Times* on CBS and John Chancellor paraphrasing the *New York Times* on NBC?

The roll call of the states droned on, but I tuned it out. I was thinking of the boy on the bicycle. The ten-year-old boy who was a little shy, a little introspective—sensitive, as Liz McCall had correctly divined—but not sick in the head. Not broken. Not yet.

Before long, that boy would change. And damn it all, I still didn't know why. I still couldn't recover the memory, couldn't get at the truth of things. The truth behind me and what I'd done, what I'd kept on doing.

It had begun with Clara and Enid's cat. Yes, Mr. Tibbs, the Siamese I'd seen on the porch. It was an autumn day—September, probably. Maybe two months from now. The cat had gotten loose and was wandering in the neighborhood. I came across him in my backyard. He was looking at me. Just looking, with his guileless blue eyes. And for no reason at all, I grabbed hold of that cat, and with a wrench of my wrists I broke his neck.

Afterward I buried him in the woods, feeling ashamed and baffled and afraid.

My parents never said anything about the missing cat. But I believe they suspected. That was probably why we moved away later that fall. A new town in a new state; a new life; a new beginning.

But not for me. The anger didn't go away. It got worse as I grew up, metastasizing like a cancer until it took over my life. I spent only two years in college before I was expelled for beating the crap out of an upperclassman. I lost my first job for a similar reason, except in that case the victim was my boss. He pressed charges. I was on probation for a while, and I had to do therapy, not that it helped.

There were other incidents, some more serious than others. Twice I've done time—a ten-month stretch, then two and a half years. I did my share of fighting in the pen. Each time I came out more damaged than before.

And on one occasion I killed a man. I never got caught for that one. I took off running, and later I read about it in the newspaper. His death shocked me. I hadn't intended to take it that far. But truthfully, in that episode or any other, I never really *intended* to do anything. I simply lost all control. Something would come over me, an itch in my palms, the red rage, mental shutdown, and on automatic pilot I would lash out, hitting as hard as I could, again and again and again ...

It's not like I did it all the time. I'd gone years without a blowup. Well, two years. Two years, seven months, and eleven days, to be precise. Yes, I'd kept track—like the alcoholic who remembers exactly how long it's been since the last time he fell off the wagon. For all that time I kept my head down, working steadily at my job and being no more antisocial than the guy in the cubicle next to me.

Oh yes, I have a job. It's not a good job—low salary, no benefits—but I do draw a paycheck. It's one of many jobs I've held throughout the course of my life. There are businesses too disorganized to conduct a thorough background check, and others too desperate for low-wage employees to snub an applicant merely for a couple of stretches in state prison.

Besides, I'm something of a charmer when I want to be. I don't come across as the violent, physical type. I'm reasonably articulate and well read, and I dress well. Frankly, I dress above my means. I wear a better wristwatch than I can afford, and my few suits are of above-average quality. Respectability counts for a lot. People are idiots; they judge a man on the most superficial things. In my younger days, there were mothers who actually tried to fix me up with their daughters. Luckily for all concerned, those matchmaking efforts failed.

My few romantic relationships have all ended badly. I've never been married. My longest entanglement lasted almost a full year before the lady called it quits, sternly informing me that I had "personal demons." Don't I know it.

All in all, I've made quite a wreck of my life. The things regular people acquire by middle age—spouse, kids, savings, a modicum of social status—have eluded me. I've made many attempts at reform. I've taken many vows to control myself, to keep my temper in check, to stop making the same stupid, crazy mistakes. But I can't help it. Whatever furious insanity is percolating inside me can be suppressed only so long before it comes boiling up, and once again my fists are skinned and bloodied.

I could tell you I have my good qualities. I give to charity. I volunteer at a hospital. I'm a quiet neighbor. If you lived next door to me, you'd never know I was there. Hell, maybe you do live next door. How well do you know your neighbors, anyway?

So, yes, I can make a case for myself. But it would be a self-serving lie. None of that other stuff matters, not in comparison to the red ink on the ledger. A thousand days of volunteer work couldn't cancel out even Clara and Enid's cat. I know that. I'm not an idiot. I'm just a crazy fuck.

But I wasn't born that way. I was made.

And maybe, just maybe, I could be unmade.

The idea, half-formed, wouldn't leave me alone. Restless, I left the house again around nine o'clock. It was fully dark by now. I retraced the familiar route along the street. I didn't anticipate running into anyone. But as it turned out, I met myself.

The boy lay on his belly on the front lawn of 114 Miller, his chin resting on his palms, watching fireflies. The glowing creatures danced for him, performing luminous arabesques in the night.

Yeah, I used to do that. Funny how I'd stopped noticing fireflies. They must still exist in 2016—they hadn't gone extinct or anything—but I hadn't seen one in years.

He noticed me watching him. I hesitated, wondering if the rules of the game allowed me to interact with my other self. I decided to find out.

"Hey, kid," I said. "Nice night."

"Yes, sir."

Sir, huh? Kids sure were polite in '72.

"This your house?"

He nodded. I asked if he liked living here. He said yes, because it was close to the beach. He liked going down to the boardwalk and getting a hot dog from the stand. I'd forgotten those hot dogs. They'd been damn good—big fat frankfurters slathered in Gulden's mustard and diced onion. There was nothing equally appealing in the Stevensons' pantry.

I didn't know what else to say to him. There was so much I could have told him about the mistakes he was fated to make, the opportunities he would squander. But the words wouldn't come, and anyway, if I'd said any of that, he would have thought I was a crazy person.

There was one thing, though. One thing I could say, even though it probably wouldn't make any difference.

"You enjoying these summer days?" I asked.

"Yeah, I guess."

"You should. You should make them last. Milk 'em for all they're worth. This is a special time in your life, kid. It'll never be like this again."

"Like what?"

"No responsibilities, no worries. No boss chewing you out, no next-door neighbor complaining about the music, no ex-girlfriend shaking you down. No lying bitch—"

I stopped myself. Way to go, using that kind of language on a ten-year-old. And in '72, no less, when the most off-color content on TV was George Gobel kibitzing with Johnny Carson on *The Tonight Show.*

"What I mean is," I went on, "right now the world's your oyster. It won't always be like that. Make the most of it."

"Okay," he said doubtfully.

I knew I hadn't made much of an impression, but I hadn't really expected to. "What'd you do today?"

"Rode my bike around. Went to the newspaper store, but there weren't any new comics. I was looking for *Spider-Man.*"

Spidey and the Hulk had been my favorites. Peter Parker and Bruce Banner—one bitten by a radioactive spider, the other exposed to a nuclear blast. Amazing what radiation could do for you in the right dosage.

"I like the Marvel ones the best," I said.

"Me, too."

"Yeah, the DC comics are too dumb, with all those fantasy episodes."

He nodded. "Like the one where Clark Kent and Lois Lane get married and have super babies."

"That one sucked," I agreed, then wondered if *sucked* was an appropriate term to use in conversation in this era.

"They're not the worst, though." He propped himself up higher on his elbows, getting into the discussion. "The worst are the funny ones, *supposedly* funny"—he drew out the four-syllable word with pedantic precision—"like *Casper* and *Richie Rich*. I had this friend stay over once, and all he wanted to read was *Archie*."

He said it with a wince of distaste. I remembered that friend, David Ridgeway, and his pathetic taste in comics. I'd made jokes about it with my other friends. Probably I'd made those jokes when David was around—right in front of him. And the rest of us had laughed.

Hey, I never said I was a saint. I was just a normal kid.

Normal. Yeah, that's the thing. In those days I was normal. A bit socially awkward, a little too introspective, but basically sane.

I had never been a normal adult. And right in this moment I knew how much I wanted to be.

It was the normality of this boy's life that I missed. It was normality that I was pleading with him to cherish and hold on to.

"I like some of the Disney ones, though," he was saying. His face brightened. "We're going to Disney World next week."

"Disney World?"

"In Florida. The new one. It's gonna be really cool."

"Yes. I'm sure it will be."

You know how, in books, the narrator will say a strange foreboding came over him? That was how I felt right then. There was no reason for it. What could be more harmless, more innocuous, than Disney World? Except...

The front door opened. "Who's out there?"

I forgot whatever I'd been thinking of. I forgot everything as I stared at the doorway that framed a tall man in a T-shirt and shorts.

I knew him. He was the man who'd taught me to play Parcheesi and Yahtzee and chess. The man who'd bought my first copy of *Playboy*. The man who'd taken me outside on the night of the Apollo 11 landing and pointed up at the moon, showing me where the astronauts walked. That man.

My father, who died of non-Hodgkin's lymphoma in 1996, at the age of sixty-five.

He was alive now. And he was ticked off.

He came down the front stoop, watching me with suspicious eyes. For the first time I noticed how much he looked like me. Or I looked like him, I guess. But he obviously didn't see it. I don't think he really took in my appearance. Besides—strange thought—I was older than he was. He had been forty-one in 1972. At fifty-four, I was thirteen years his senior.

"Do I know you?" he asked.

The answer to that question was a great deal more complicated than he could have imagined.

"John Walker," I said, sticking out my hand, which he ignored. The name sounded awfully phony to me. I wished I'd picked a better one.

"Live around here?" he asked.

I repeated my story about staying with friends one town over. He seemed unconvinced. He wanted to know what I'd been talking to his son about.

"Comic books," I said.

"That's true, Dad," the boy said.

His father—*my* father—paid no attention. "I don't like him talking to strangers."

"Sorry. I didn't mean any harm."

Behind him, a female figure appeared at the screen door, a silhouette against an ambient glow. I recognized her well enough, even an outline. I suppose you never forget your mother, do you?

She, too, was dead—dead in the reality of 2016, I mean. She had suffered a fatal heart attack three years after my father passed. My last look at her had been when she lay in an open casket. I'd kissed her embalmed forehead. It was cold, like stone.

And now there she was, watching us from a few yards away. A faceless shape haloed in light. Like those deceased loved ones you're supposed to see at the end of a tunnel when you die.

So close to me. I could walk right up to that door and give her a hug.

I didn't, of course. I was pretty sure dear old Dad wouldn't care for that.

"I guess I'm coming on a little strong," he said to me half-apologetically. "But lately we've had some trouble in this town."

The break-ins seemed to have everyone on edge.

"I heard about that," I said. "I hope they catch the guy."

"They'll catch him." He looked hard at me, perhaps intending the statement as a warning. "Well ... nice meeting you."

It was a dismissal. I said good-night and moved on. When I glanced back, I saw my father and mother looking after me, but the boy on the lawn had already returned to watching fireflies.

V

MY INTERVIEW WITH myself left me unsettled. Rattled, even. I wasn't sure why. To take the edge off, I indulged in some of Mr. Stevenson's scotch. By midnight I was pretty mellow. I commandeered one of the twin beds in the master bedroom and fell asleep reading a paperback I found on the night table. The book was *The Exorcist (#1 Bestseller, The Shocker of the Year!)*, and the cover price was $1.75. There was no TV in the bedroom, so *The Exorcist* was my only entertainment option, other than masturbation.

Okay, yeah, I did that, too.

I read with a flashlight, not wanting any lights to be visible in the windows. It gave me kind of a cozy feeling, like when I'd hidden under the covers secretly reading a sci-fi book or a comic, long after my parents believed I'd gone to sleep. Maybe my other self was doing the same thing half a block away.

I dozed off with the book in my hand, the flashlight off. Around five AM, I awoke. I lay there, staring into the predawn darkness. I knew what had gotten me worked up. It was Disney World.

The boy had said he was going there next week. Big family trip. High anticipation.

But he would never take that trip. The vacation would be canceled at the last minute. I remembered that much. But as for why it would be canceled ...

A blank space. Amnesiac gap.

Whatever was due to happen to me this summer must have taken place just before our scheduled departure for

Florida. Which meant it would happen sometime in the next few days.

Tomorrow, possibly. Or over the weekend.

Soon.

I got up. I paced the house. My mind hummed with electric urgency. I felt I was on the trail of something big.

This long, lazy summer, this summer of Nixon and McGovern, fireflies and sultry nights and hot dogs on the boardwalk, would be the last normal part of my life. And the boy who had rested on the lawn chatting about Spider-Man would never be the same again. In a day or two, his life would take an irrevocable wrong turn; the tracks would be switched, the train rerouted into dark territory.

And here I was, transported by some incomprehensible magic to this year, to this month, almost to the very day. It couldn't be coincidence. There had to be a purpose behind it.

I was on a mission of redemption. I'd been sent here to set things right.

I knew of only one way to do it. It involved a supposition. Clara and Enid believed the antisocial Mr. Wilson was responsible for the rash of burglaries. And the break-ins were getting closer to Miller Avenue.

When I'd read the newspaper story, I'd felt instinctively that it had something to do with me. Now I had a working hypothesis.

Okay, follow me on this. Let's say Mr. Wilson really was the housebreaker with a fetish for ladies' underwear. Let's say he was soon to break into the house at 114 Miller, directly across the street from the place he was renting. Let's say the little boy in that house would be home at the time.

You with me so far?

Something more would have to happen. I couldn't be sure what it was. But I could make an educated guess. I remembered how Mr. Wilson had watched me and the other kids from his window. The unhealthy interest on his face.

If he was destined to attack me, molest me—well, it would explain everything. The repressed memory, the post-traumatic symptoms, the violent episodes. The full catastrophe, in Zorba the Greek's memorable phrase.

You're saying, sure, nice story, but what if I was wrong?

I could be, obviously. Mr. Wilson might not be the burglar at all. The police hadn't been impressed with Enid's theory. Maybe they were right to be skeptical.

Maybe not.

The police needed a warrant to search someone's home. I didn't. I could break in later today, while Mr. Wilson was at work. I could toss his place. If he had a stash of stolen lingerie, I'd find it.

And if I did ...

Then I would make sure he never got the chance to trespass in our house.

It all seemed incredibly unlikely, from one standpoint—yet persuasively simple, from another. I felt I had been delivered here for a reason, then led by the hand to understand what I had to do. I'd been offered a chance to unmake the disaster of my life and save the boy I had been from becoming the man I was now.

A chance to undo every crime, and to make everything right.

vi

NATURALLY I COULDN'T get back to sleep. With hours to go before I could risk entering the Wilson place, I lugged the Stevensons' 8mm projector out of the closet and treated myself to a selection of their home movies. Yeah, that's how starved I was for entertainment. The absence of HBO, Netflix, and Turner Classic Movies was hitting me hard. And I wasn't really getting into *The Exorcist*. The story held no surprises. I'd already seen the movie, even though it wouldn't come out till next year.

Around eight AM, I fixed breakfast. Sometimes daylight brings second thoughts and new doubts, but not in this case. My purpose was clear.

Upstairs, I took another luxuriously wasteful 1970s shower, then attired myself in bell-bottom jeans and a bright orange shirt. Orange, never my favorite color, seemed to enjoy an unhealthy popularity right now.

Before setting out, I strapped on my Fossil watch and stuffed my cell phone and wallet into my pants pockets. If things went as planned, I intended to go straight to Ground Zero again, and with my mission accomplished, I fully expected to be zipped home. The '70s duds wouldn't look so groovy in the twenty-first century, but I still needed camouflage here.

Admittedly I was getting ahead of myself. Before I started making travel plans, I had to find out if Mr. Wilson was my white whale, or only a red herring.

Hey, that's clever. Let me write that down.

I slipped out the side door and went along the inlet, skirting other backyards, until I reached the house Mr.

Wilson was renting. It was after ten by now, and he was off doing whatever he did during business hours.

Once again I was faced with the necessity of breaking into a house on Miller Avenue. This time I wanted to leave no evidence of forced entry. I'd brought along a kitchen knife, flathead screwdriver, and rubber mallet scavenged from the Stevenson place. Needing extra cargo capacity for these items, I'd donned a light summer jacket in a giraffe pattern. Yeah. Giraffe. I wasn't really sure if it belonged to Mr. or Mrs. Stevenson, but it had deep pockets.

Mr. Wilson's house, like all the houses on the street, had a rear patio accessed by a sliding door. I'd already decided to go in that way.

Even a locked sliding door is easy to open. Here's your tutorial, boys and girls. First comes the screen door. Just lift off the track with the knife until the whole door pops free. To defeat the glass door, lever your screwdriver under the latch and tap the handle with the hammer. It should take only two or three blows to do the job.

Not that I recommend breaking and entering, of course. It's against the law.

And also, don't do drugs.

Okay, so I made it in. I was wearing gloves, by the way—white cotton gloves courtesy of Mrs. Stevenson. Kind of fay, I admit, but easier to work with than the heavy black leather gloves favored by her husband. Anyway, they seemed to go with the jacket.

The gloves were a fail-safe option. If I succeeded in going home, it wouldn't matter if my prints were found. But if I failed—well, there wouldn't be many places to hide from the law as long as I was restricted to a single block.

Now for the treasure hunt. I started with the bedroom, the most obvious hiding place. Closet, bureau, nightstand, and under the bed itself. No luck.

On to more imaginative locations. Inside the freezer and refrigerator. Behind furniture. In the garage. Still nothing.

I was beginning to think the neighborhood gossip was wrong, and Mr. Wilson was just a harmless weirdo. Either that, or he was making his own private contribution to women's lib by burning the bras he stole.

And then, just like that, I found them. I'd made the mistake of assuming I was up against a criminal mastermind, or at least an ordinarily competent thief. It turned out Mr. Wilson was neither. He'd made no special effort to hide his collection. The bras, panties, and stockings lay, neatly sorted, in a laundry hamper.

Apparently they had been recently washed and not yet put away. I supposed he needed to wash them pretty often, given the likely purpose for which they'd been collected.

So now I knew what I had to do. To stop Mr. Wilson from ruining my life, I had to prevent him from breaking into 114 Miller Avenue.

Which meant I had to kill the sad little son of a bitch.

Hey, what did you expect? My whole future was at stake. It was no time for half measures. Besides, given what I now knew, terminating this pervert was a simple act of self-defense.

I wasn't looking forward to it. In all previous cases, I'd acted on impulse while out of control. This time I would be in full possession of my faculties. And I wasn't just going to administer a beating. I would be committing murder—cold-blooded, premeditated.

What's that *Hamlet* thing? The time is out of joint. O cursed spite, that ever I was born to set it right.

Like it or not, I had no intention of putting it off any longer than necessary. Idleness is the devil's playground, you know. And people like Robin Williams and Oprah are always telling us to seize the day. Besides, who knew when Captain Underpants might get it into his head to burglarize our house? It could be any time.

So I would do the job this evening, when he got home. And I would make it look like suicide.

Another fail-safe option. In the event that the barrier at Ground Zero wasn't lifted, Mr. Wilson's death had to be an open-and-shut case. I didn't need the police asking a lot of troublesome questions.

I knotted together two of the nylon stockings from the hamper to make a noose. The living room was my choice for the ambush site. There was a hook in the ceiling meant for a hanging plant, but left conveniently unused. Directly under it was a small coffee table. Both would serve my purposes admirably.

Happily for me, Mr. Wilson was a reclusive man, the type who always kept his curtains drawn. The room would be dark enough to offer concealment, and no one outdoors would see what went on inside.

After that, I waited. Rain fell intermittently throughout the day. The drumbeat of drops on the roof was soothing. More than once I almost fell asleep.

In my drowsy state I contemplated the possible implications of success in my venture. Having rewritten my past, I presumably would have erased my future—the future that had resulted in me as I was right now. Would I wink out of existence, replaced by another edition of me, a parallel-universe version who was married with children, a safe, boring man who never got blood on his hands? Would the price of redemption be the extinction of the ego I knew as myself?

If so, it was a price I was willing to pay. Nonexistence wasn't the worst fate I could imagine. It was, in all honesty, probably better than I deserved.

But I didn't really think it would play out that way. I expected to return to 2016 as myself, but without the compulsions that had driven me. I would be me, but healed. Me 2.0. A new man. A normal man. That was my hope.

Shortly after five PM, Mr. Wilson parked in the garage and came up the back stairs. As he entered the living room,

I caught him on the back of the head with the mallet, hard enough to drop him in a heap. That was the theory, anyway. But you know what some famous general said: No plan of action ever survives first contact with the enemy.

Mr. Wilson was the hardheaded type. He staggered but didn't fall. I flung the noose around his neck and wrenched it tight. He had to die by strangulation. I'd meant to do it while he was unconscious, but he hadn't left me that option.

I wrestled with him as he clawed at the nylon. He was stronger than he looked—small but compactly built, like a bantamweight fighter, with a low center of gravity that made him hard to bring down—and he fought desperately like the cornered animal he was.

A choked scream struggled to escape from his throat. I held on to the noose with one hand, while with the other I clapped his mouth shut. That was a mistake. The bastard bit my hand, drawing blood.

I believe I may have said the f-word. I was getting mad now. Some people just don't know how to die.

With my foot hooked under his leg, I tipped him off balance, and the two of us went down together. He still wouldn't quit, God damn him. We tussled on the floor, rolling over and over as I fought to maintain my grip on the noose. He kicked out at the carpet and propelled us into the coffee table, overturning it. An ashtray and a succession of heavy books, later determined to be the Time-Life series *This Fabulous Century*, thumped on my shoulder blades. If any of them had conked me on the head, I might have been the one to get KO'd.

My energy was fading. I needed to end this thing fast. With a last effort I shoved his face into the deep shag carpet, pinning him down with a knee on the back of his neck. I twisted the noose tighter. With his throat constricted and his nose and mouth smushed against the rug, he couldn't breathe. His fists pounded the floor. He spasmed, his mouth frothing, and lay still.

I straddled him for another minute, just to be sure he wasn't shamming. A guy as stubborn as this one might have more than one life in him.

But no. He was all done, thank God.

I got up slowly, breathing hard. Random lights flashed across my field of vision, and parts of me felt numb and tingly. I thought this would be a very bad time to have a heart attack.

I looked down at him. He was all twisted on the carpet. He looked impossibly small. How he had held out so long against me, I didn't know. Things hadn't gone as planned, that was for sure. I'd never strangled anyone before, and I can't say I liked it.

I inspected my palm. The bite wasn't too bad. I wiped off the blood and rinsed it under hot water in the bathroom, then applied antiseptic and a Band-Aid. The wound would heal. I ought to be all right, unless Mr. Wilson had rabies. The way the little scrote had fought, I couldn't rule it out.

When my breathing was back to normal, I arranged the crime scene. I left the coffee table overturned where it was and dragged Mr. Wilson directly underneath the ceiling hook. I was careful to tear a long rip in the nylon at its free end.

Get the picture? He'd tried to hang himself, but at some point during the ordeal, after he'd kicked over the coffee table and was dangling and choking, the nylon had torn free of the hook, and he'd hit the floor. This explained the bump on his noggin and any other injuries he'd sustained. Evidently the stocking had been pulled tight enough to finish the job as he lay half-conscious, clawing reflexively at the noose.

There was no need for a suicide note. Many people don't leave them. The fact that he'd used a pair of his fetish items as the instruments of his death would be enough to suggest his state of mind. He was sickened by his unhealthy obsessions, or something. Anyway, no one would be too concerned about the self-inflicted demise of a housebreaker and a friendless sicko. And the days of CSI investigations were still a long way off. I wasn't worried about DNA evidence or microscopic contamination of the crime scene.

I took care of these details with methodical efficiency. I had no regrets about killing Mr. Wilson. To tell you the truth, I was feeling uncommonly good about things. I had done it, really *done* it. I had preempted my childhood trauma, altered the trajectory of my life.

It took all my willpower to linger in the house for another three hours, until darkness had fallen. I didn't want to risk being seen in daylight as I left. I was still thinking in fail-safe terms.

You might assume it was creepy to hang out with the body of the man I'd just murdered, but to be honest, I was okay with it. Corpses are pretty boring. It's not as if they're going to rise up and take revenge. They just lie there, looking dead.

Please don't judge me—well, not more than you already have—but with empty hours to fill, I found myself feeling a bit peckish. So I noshed on some of Mr. Wilson's comestibles. Sliced turkey, rye bread, a dab of mayo. I ate all of it—no leftovers to raise questions for the police—and washed the plate and knife before putting them away.

Mr. Wilson's TV was bigger and better than the Stevensons', though the reception was just as iffy. I watched the news. McGovern, McGovern, McGovern. Skyjacking. Spiro Agnew blasted "radical chic elitists." The Dow Jones Industrial Average closed at 916. My advice: buy.

I reset the screen door on its track and relocked the glass door. After nine o'clock, I finally slipped out through another exit. The white gloves, along with the knife, screwdriver, and mallet, went into the inlet behind Mr. Wilson's house. The tools sank, and the gloves floated away like lily pads.

I wondered how long it would be before Mr. Wilson was discovered. It seemed unlikely anyone would to investigate his disappearance for at least a few days. By then, he would be pretty ripe. And—fingers crossed—I would be gone.

I made my way along the inlet until I drew within fifty feet of First Avenue. I wanted to approach Ground Zero from the middle of the street, retracing the route I'd followed when I entered, so I cut through a vacant lot where we kids had played ball on summer days. Pickup games, blessedly free of adult supervision. No helicopter parents in this era, and no trophies for coming in second. No trophies at all, in fact.

There were things about this moment in history that I would actually miss. But not enough to hold me here. Because, let's face it, I simply had no future in 1972.

The street was empty. As I headed toward the intersection at a brisk clip, I scrolled through a mental inventory. Wristwatch? Check. Phone? Check. Wallet? Check.

It looked like I was good to go.

I would just keep walking straight ahead until I found myself back on that rainswept city street. What happened after that ...

Well, nothing would happen. There would be no cops chasing me, because I would have committed no crime, because in the future I'd just made, I wasn't a twisted fuck with a hair-trigger temper. I wasn't a wanted man or a hunted animal. I was ...

Truthfully, I didn't know what I was, or would be, but I was more than a little interested to find out.

When I was fifty feet away from the intersection, I felt the first nudge of resistance.

I told myself it was my imagination. But it was a poor lie, one I couldn't sell even to myself. With every step, the invisible force of repulsion increased. Just as before, the street sucked at my shoes, the stretch of asphalt clinging to me like I was a mammoth in a tar pit. I advanced another few struggling steps, then a half step, and then I was frozen in place, a yard from the end of the curb, unable to proceed.

Still trapped in 1972. Still confined to one block of Miller Avenue. Even now, with Mr. Wilson dead in his house.

I retreated, withdrawing from the intersection until I could walk normally and breathe freely again.

Then I sat down on the curb, alone and invisible in the dark, and buried my head in my hands.

And wept.

vii

IT TOOK ME a long time to pull myself together. I might have stayed there all night if it hadn't started to rain again. A light rain, barely more than a mist, but it got me moving down the middle of the street in the general direction of the Stevenson house, which I was still obliged to call home.

"Mr. Walker ...!"

Liz McCall's voice. I turned, and there she was, on her front porch. Did everyone sit out on porches in the summer of '72?

"May I offer shelter from the storm?" she added.

I was in no mood to talk, but I couldn't very well refuse. It would look downright suspicious.

So I took cover under the overhang and we chatted for a bit, or rather, she chatted and I half listened. She was still dressed in her work outfit, a checkered pantsuit that looked disconcertingly like pajamas. I noticed she raised an eyebrow at the giraffe jacket, confirming my suspicion that it belonged to Mrs. Stevenson.

She said she'd been watching the convention, but it had become so chaotic that McGovern's acceptance speech had been indefinitely delayed. She wasn't sure when or if he would get to speak. Even so, she thought McGovern had a real shot at an upset in November. I didn't have the heart to disillusion her.

She was all about optimism and thinking good thoughts. She quoted—actually quoted—from *Jonathan Livingston Seagull*, a bestseller that year, which she was currently reading. It certainly made an interesting contrast to *The Exorcist*.

After a while I found myself relaxing. Somehow I'd managed to put Ground Zero out of my mind. I was actually enjoying myself, and so when she invited me inside for a cup of Sanka, I said yes.

I followed her into her tiny kitchen with its ugly linoleum floor and bright yellow Formica countertops and a *Jesus Christ Superstar* poster tacked to the wall. She heated water on the stove, poured it into a couple of mugs in psychedelic colors, and stirred in some freeze-dried granules. She was still talking about that damn seagull and the important message he had for the new generation.

"We need to have hope," she said, "for the children."

"Like a boy you babysit for?" I asked. Oh, yes, I'm very sly.

She nodded, giving his name and asking if I knew his parents. I said no, which was true in one respect, and, in another respect, the biggest fib I'd ever told.

We were sitting in a room off the kitchen by then, at a small round table covered in a vinyl tablecloth with a ladybug print. She'd turned on a portable radio, a bulky Panasonic with three big knobs and a wide metal handle. "Starman" by David Bowie played softly.

"You remind me of that boy," she said thoughtfully.

I hadn't expected her to pick up on that. "Do I?"

"There's something about you. About the eyes ..." She studied me almost provocatively, then looked away. "I don't know what it is."

I knew, of course. But I wasn't telling. "You like this kid, I take it."

"Very much. That's why I sit with him. It's not really about the money. It's just that I have no children of my own, and ... Well, you know how it is for a woman."

I thought I did. I also thought no woman of my day would put it just like that.

"You don't need children to complete you," I said. "Or a man."

She laughed. "You sound like Gloria Steinem."

"It's true, though."

"Is it? I don't know. I would have had kids, if Mark had hung around."

"Mark?"

"My ex-husband. We were talking about it. But he decided he'd rather run off with my best friend. Who, I guess, didn't turn out to be such a good friend, after all."

"I'm sorry."

"It happens." She said it too glibly, and the hand holding the coffee cup shook a little. "I'm all right."

"You could remarry."

"I'm getting a little long in the tooth for that."

She was maybe thirty-five. Not my idea of long in the tooth. Then again, a divorced woman in her mid-thirties might be a tough sell in Hugh Hefner's world.

My brief visit was turning out to be a lot longer than expected, but I was in no hurry to leave. I liked Liz, but it was more than that. I felt comfortable around her. I felt almost ... normal. No conflicting feelings, no suppressed anger, no ticking time bomb or sputtering fuse. Maybe I really had rewritten my future somehow. Even if I was still detained here, maybe my compulsions were gone.

We went into the living room, where she kept a phonograph. She dropped a stack of LPs on the turntable, classic rock that hadn't had time to become classic yet. She snuggled up next to me, and as Cat Stevens was crooning "Morning Has Broken," she asked if I ever smoked pot.

"It's been a while," I said.

"Want to smoke some now?"

It really had been a long time since I'd done any '70s weed. Well—since the '70s, come to think of it. So I said yes.

She rolled a couple of joints, proving quite skillful at it, and we lit up. The sweetish aroma of marijuana slowly filled the room in wisps of smoke. We sat there getting high and grooving to Simon and Garfunkel, the Doors, the Supremes, Joni Mitchell. There was also Gary Glitter, who was a bit of a buzzkill. She kept the volume low, and we talked in the aimless way that potheads do. It was all very mellow. I felt as if I'd walked into the last season of *Mad Men*.

The subject of Clara and Enid came up. She confided in me that they were not actually sisters. Evidently she thought it was a well-kept secret. "Such a shame they have to hide their love, when there's not enough love in the world as it is. Why must society be like that?"

I suggested that attitudes would change. People like Clara and Enid would be more open about their relationships. Eventually, it would even be legal to marry someone of the same sex.

"Sure it will," she said with a roll of her eyes.

"All kinds of barriers will come down."

"I suppose we'll have a woman president, too."

"Well ... maybe not."

She sighed. "I don't know. Other countries have done it. Indira Gandhi, Golda Meir ... But first we need to elect McGovern."

"McGovern will lose," I said. "Nixon will carry forty-nine states."

"Not a chance."

"But he won't serve out his second term. He'll resign, and Gerald Ford will be president."

"Who's Gerald Ford?"

"Vice-president."

"That's Agnew."

"Agnew will have resigned already."

"You have a vivid imagination, Mr. Walker."

"That's not my real name."

"No? What is it?"

"Han Solo."

"That's not even a name. Try again."

"Barack Obama."

She giggled. "I don't think that one's a name, either."

"You'd be surprised what the future holds."

"So you're an expert on the future?"

I felt like telling her that I'd gotten unstuck in time, like Vonnegut's Billy Pilgrim. She would have found it funny. At the moment, so did I.

"I *am* an expert," I said sententiously. "I'm your magic eight-ball. Ask me anything."

"Will we have hotels in orbit and a moon colony, like in *2001*?"

"No, but we'll have Netflix and Snapchat and YouTube and Google."

"You sound like Dr. Seuss." She giggled again. "There'll be floobles and strooples and oodles of noodles ..."

"Just wait and see. It won't be anything like you think. No jetpacks, but there'll be drones. No robot butlers, but there'll be robot vacuum cleaners. No hologram shows, but there'll be flatscreen TVs with two hundred channels to choose from. Including porn."

"Pornography? On television? They won't even let you say the c-word."

"The c-word?" There was only one c-word I knew, but I didn't think she meant that one.

"You know." She shrugged. "Crap."

"Oh ... Believe me, crap is the least of it. There'll be songs on the radio that sound like cases of Tourette syndrome. Movies and video games that will drop you smack in the middle of a bloodbath."

"What are video games?"

I wasn't listening. I'd become mesmerized by the monotone of my own voice.

"It's a rougher, coarser society in some ways. Nobody dresses up anymore. We all look like slobs. Fat, too. An epidemic of fatness. Too much junk food, too many carbs. We're complacent and lazy and easily offended and constantly outraged by the stupidest things. And we spend way too much time looking at pictures of cats."

"Doesn't sound very appealing. I thought the future was supposed to be Shangri-La."

"No utopia. War and more war."

"The war won't last forever. Once Nixon's out—"

"Nixon or no Nixon, it makes no difference. There'll always be wars and rumors of wars. But not World War III. We'll dodge that bullet. The Berlin Wall will come down without firing a shot."

"I don't think Brezhnev will allow that."

"People will take sledgehammers to the damn thing and sell the rubble as souvenirs. And everyone will think it's the end of history, all problems solved. But that's before the terrorists."

"In Northern Ireland?"

"In Afghanistan and Syria and—well, everywhere. They'll bring down the World Trade Center."

"The Twin Towers are barely even up, and already you want to knock them down?"

"I don't want to. I just know what's coming."

"Bad Moon rising," she said dreamily, a sleepy, goofy smile riding her lips.

It was true. Al Qaeda and ISIS, Chernobyl and Three Mile Island, the Munich Olympics and the Iran hostages, double-digit inflation and the stock market crash, AIDS and Ebola, Ted Bundy and Jeffrey Dahmer—yes, a bad moon on the rise.

I felt sorry for her, then. I felt sorry for us all.

"Shouldn't have talked like this," I mumbled. "Didn't mean to bring you down."

She only laughed. "I didn't take it seriously. The World Trade Center—you couldn't knock over those skyscrapers with an atom bomb."

"No, they'll stand forever," I agreed. "They'll outlast us all."

It was better to lie. Easier, too. So I told her about the future as it would *really* be. The future I knew she wanted. No war, no poverty, no racism or injustice. A spiritual awakening, a new sense of oneness with each other and with the planet, an endless idyll of universal peace.

She ate it up. She really was one of the Eloi. She didn't even believe in the Morlocks, when you got right down to it. To her, all the evil in the world was only a scary story told around the campfire. She saw no true darkness in anyone—not even me.

Around midnight, I became aware of where the evening was headed. This was the swinging '70s, after all, the time of key parties and free love, porn-star mustaches and *Bob and Carol and Ted and Alice.* A heyday of guilt-free promiscuity, an erotic eruption after decades of repression. The party was just getting started. Morning had broken, all right.

She was on the pill and didn't so much as suggest that I use a condom, which was good because I didn't have one, and I hardly could have made a drugstore run. Why worry, though? HIV wasn't even an acronym yet.

We went into the bedroom. She was warm and soft in the dark, and she breathed low moans in my ear.

And I learned there was another thing I liked about women in this era. They hadn't read a million *Redbook* articles on the perfect orgasm. They didn't expect you to be a sexual triathlete or a gym rat with six-pack abs and zero percent body fat. I'd forgotten what it was like to perform my manly duties without worrying about how I stacked up against an *Oprah* magazine spread or Hugh Jackman's latest screen incarnation. I already knew I wasn't going to rock anybody's Casbah, but in 1972 I didn't have to.

It was good. I mean—well, obviously it was good, but it felt more than just ordinarily good. It felt like the first phase of my redemption, the first normal relationship I'd enjoyed in many years, or maybe ever.

I wondered if the gate at Ground Zero had remained barred to me because I'd been meant to experience this night, this intimacy. Whatever higher power was orchestrating my journey of repentance seemed to have a few more tricks up its sleeve.

Or maybe not. It seemed unlikely that the dimensions of time and space had been mystically fine-tuned for a booty call.

This observation struck me as humorous, and I'm pretty sure I fell asleep with a smile on my face.

viii

I'M NOT THE type to walk out on a woman in the middle of the night. I may be scum, but I'm not that kind of scum. Besides, I was secretly hoping for another ride on the merry-go-round before breakfast.

But it was not to be. When I awoke in her bed that morning, she was already gone. A note on the kitchen table said she was off to work, and that I could fix myself breakfast if I wished.

Her fridge offered milk and eggs, delicacies the Stevensons had denied me. I was frying up two of the eggs when the phone rang. I hesitated about answering. This wasn't my house, and maybe Liz wouldn't want anyone knowing a man was here. But I could always say it was a wrong number.

"John? I'm glad you picked up." She was phoning from work. Rather shyly, she asked if I would use the back door when leaving the house. She'd forgotten to mention it in her note, but—well, it would be best that way.

Liz McCall might be hip and liberated, but she still had a reputation to maintain.

Naturally I agreed. She was about to ring off when she remembered something else.

"Have you heard the news? No, of course you haven't. Mr. Wilson—the man everyone thought was the burglar? Well, he really *was*. And now ... he's dead."

Breathlessly she summarized events. Police cars had been parked along the street when she was leaving. She'd stopped to ask Clara and Enid about it. They'd already spoken to the cops. They knew everything.

It seemed Mr. Wilson had fallen behind with the rent. His landlord, showing up early this morning to catch him before work, had discovered him dead on the floor. Mr. Wilson had taken his own life. Details were sketchy, but he was definitely confirmed as the sneak thief with an underwear fetish, and he was definitely dead.

I made the appropriate comments. When the call was over, I ate my eggs. The news had not affected my appetite in the least.

True, it was a surprise that the body had been discovered so soon, but I couldn't see that it would matter. I only needed to lie low until the police were gone from the area.

I collected my—or rather, Mrs. Stevenson's—giraffe jacket and left via the back door so as not to besmirch Mrs. McCall's honor. I was careful to avoid being spotted as I made my way along the inlet to the Stevenson place.

Inside, I was restless, anxious. The morning was warm and mostly clear, and I wanted to be outside in the summer sun. Since that wasn't an option, I contented myself with more of my hosts' scotch. It wasn't my brand, but I'd gotten to like it.

I didn't know why I felt like drinking. Maybe because things with Liz had happened faster than I could have expected. Faster than I'd wanted, even. If everything had gone according to plan, I would already have made my exit from the *All in the Family* era. Instead I was Liz McCall's boyfriend, or something. It created complications that I wasn't sure how to handle. It made me feel nervous and trapped. So I drank.

And I dozed, sliding in and out of consciousness while sprawled in the armchair in the living room.

Hours later, I was roused by a ringing doorbell.

Warily I peeked through a slit in the curtains. Two men stood at the door. One was a cop in uniform. The other wore a suit, but he was a cop also. I could tell. I can always tell.

The doorbell chimed with desultory insistence a few more times. Finally they left.

I was wide awake by now. I couldn't figure out why they would come here. It had to have something to do with the late Mr. Wilson, but I didn't see why a suicide would oblige the police to canvass the neighborhood. Unless ... unless something had gone wrong.

I wandered the house, too distracted to shower or change. At one point I caught a glimpse of myself in a mirror. I was a rumpled mess, my hair standing up in all directions, my cheeks fuzzed with stubble. It occurred to me that even before my inevitable eviction from the Stevenson place, I was already beginning to resemble one of the pond rats. And that gave me an idea.

I left the house and went through the woods to Trouble Pond, then ambled along the rocks until I found a handful of crabbers sitting and smoking. I chose one who sat apart from the rest, a nut-brown old codger with nicotine-yellowed teeth and skin the texture of dried fruit. Perched on a granite outcrop near him, I watched the water, trying not to look over my shoulder at the half-dozen patrol cars half a block away.

"A lot of activity on this street today," I ventured after a long stretch of silence.

The guy nodded. "Fella a few houses down thataway was found dead and deceased."

"So I heard. Killed himself, I understand."

"Nope. Was murdered."

This caught me up short. I tried to sound nonchalant. "Oh? What makes you say that?"

"Not me what's saying it. It's the police. My sister Jackie, she works over at the municipal building. That's cheek by jowl with the police station. She knows everything what goes on."

"Really?"

He nodded again, then spat. Plainly he was settling in

for a good bit of expository dialogue, which was fine by me. It was what I'd come for, after all.

"It was s'posed to come across as a suicide. Dead man was laid out on the floor. Made to look like he hung hisself with his stolen nylons, and the stockin's didn't hold."

"Okay."

"But the police, they say the hook in the ceiling could never've took a man's weight. Was only screwed into the plaster. Would've popped loose before the stockin's could rip. So, had to've been a setup. Whole thing was faked."

"Huh," I said, thinking that it never paid to underestimate the authorities, even if there was no CSI.

He spat again. "Sloppy job, you ask me. Lieutenant Columbo could see through it in no time."

I was about to ask if Lieutenant Columbo was a local detective. Then I remembered. Peter Falk. Right.

"They have any idea who'd want to do it?" I asked.

"Well, the neighbors do talk about this one fella. Been seen coming and going, past couple days. No one knows much about him. Said to be a strange one. Spoke to one of the neighborhood kids way too friendly, they say."

Oh, yeah. This was getting better and better.

"Huh," I said again, unimaginatively.

"Calls hisself John Walker. Sounds made up, don't it?"

"Could be."

He gave me a sidelong look, inspecting me for the first time. A hint of doubt was discernible in the furrow of his brow. "What'd you say your name was?"

"Tom Hanks." I stuck out my hand. "Pleased to know you."

I departed before his suspicions could firm up.

ix

NOW YOU'RE PROBABLY thinking that things had gotten about as bad as they could get. I thought so too.

You know what? We're both idiots.

As I headed back through the woods, I heard voices from the Stevensons' backyard. I ducked low in the brush and crept closer.

Three of the boys in blue—and in 1972, they did seem to be all boys—were congregating by the window I'd broken.

"Noticed it when I was combing the woods," one of them was saying. I didn't know what he'd been looking for, but it was probably the elusive Mr. Walker. "Figured it could be more of Wilson's work."

"You say Chuck's got a key?" another man asked.

"Yeah. The owners asked him to keep an eye on it. They're in Europe or someplace."

"So get hold of Chuck, or do you want to go through the window?"

"We already called him. He's on his way."

Shit, and double shit.

I knew what would happen next. Good old Chuck would arrive with the fabled key, and the cops would go inside and quickly discover that the house had been recently occupied. Not by the Stevensons, who were known to be away, but by a squatter, someone with a taste for scotch—I'd left the bottle out, alongside a glass of melted ice. The scotch wasn't Johnnie Walker, but I reckoned they would make the connection anyway.

I'd lost my only shelter. On the plus side, having never

changed my clothes, I still had my wallet with me, along with my cell phone and digital watch. I was all set to resume life in 2016, even if I was dressed like a backup singer for the Partridge Family.

None of which would matter if I couldn't click my ruby slippers together and go home.

Moving with what I hoped was stealth, I withdrew deeper into the woods. Since one cop had already come through here, I was trusting that no one would think to check again. Anyway, I had no other place to go.

Not until after dark. Then I would make another run at Ground Zero. By then, maybe my friends in high places would have elected to set me free.

I wasn't hopeful. But there was nothing else to do. Either I got out of 1972 tonight, or I was sure to be found tomorrow. A wanted man couldn't hide for long on a single block of a dead-end street. Besides, by tomorrow I would be getting hungry.

Hell, I was hungry now.

Nothing I could do about it. I settled down in the gully, wishing I still had the ridiculous giraffe jacket to protect me from the horseflies, and I waited.

~~~

IT WAS A long afternoon.

The day was hot. It rained once, a warm rain that soaked through me as I hunkered down amid the spike grass and sea lavender. After the rain, I became a magnet for a million mosquitoes. They fed on me with obscene gluttony, getting drunk on my blood. Had there been this many mosquitoes in my childhood? I'd forgotten them entirely. In my memory, prior to the trauma, every summer day was sun and play and laughter. A span of perfection, a last lingering taste of paradise. But that recollection was proving no more reliable than any other.

By now the whole neighborhood must be talking about me. Clara and Enid would be having quite a time of it, recounting the day they'd shared lemonade with a homicidal maniac. No doubt I became more conspicuously terrifying in each new iteration of the tale. At least Clara would have a new favorite story to replace her Asbury Park adventure.

And Liz ... I wondered what she would think. Would she believe the gossip, or would she insist I wasn't the type to commit murder?

I hoped she would stand by me, even though she would be wrong. I liked to think there would be someone in my corner. But it was more likely that she would ask herself what exactly John Walker had been doing outside at ten o'clock at night, walking in the rain.

Anyway, it didn't matter. The police wouldn't be convinced by character references. If they got hold of me, they'd have a man with no known past, no place of residence, no credit cards or bank account, no occupation, no official existence at all. Anything I told them would be an obvious lie. And the truth would be the most obvious lie of all. No one would believe I was a future edition of my boyhood self, on loan from 2016. Even I hardly believed it.

Time passed as I lay among the rushes, feeding the insect horde. Clouds crossed the sky. Streamers of sun blazed through gaps in the cloud cover, setting the tall grasses agleam.

Once or twice I heard sounds of human beings uncomfortably close by. Some kids hung out down by the water, not far from my hiding place; they had a radio with them, tuned to a station that played "Puppy Love" by Donny Osmond and "Seaside Shuffle" by Terry Dactyl and the Dinosaurs. Not all the songs from 1972 were destined to be classics.

Another time I was alarmed by the bark of a dog. The damn thing might have caught my scent; I could hear it snuffling in the brush. I worried that it was a police dog until a child's voice called out, "Tiger, get back here!" Lily O'Keefe and her sheepdog. Tiger must have obeyed. I didn't hear from him again.

I spent the rest of my time communing with God in a Zen-like meditative state. Yeah, bullshit. I spent my time feeling sick to my stomach and trembling all over like a hunted rabbit. Lying in the gully, assailed by insects, alternately sweating and rained on, hungry and helpless to do anything about it—well, I started to lose it. I mean, seriously lose it.

The whole thing was just too much. The entire situation. Somehow, until this afternoon, I'd been able to keep it together. By some trick of the mind I'd persuaded myself that what had happened to me wasn't too mind-blowingly weird. It was something I could label—a cosmic glitch or a heavenly intervention. But those were just words. The truth was, nothing made any sense. I'd been flung back in time to a summer when I was ten years old. My dead parents were alive, and so was the cat I'd killed. Nixon was president, Vietnam was at war, and according to the newspaper ads, a can of tuna fish cost forty-nine cents.

It couldn't have happened. I began to think my initial suspicion had been correct. I was hallucinating in a coma, or I was dead and in hell. Because surely if there was a hell, I belonged there, and it could hardly be much worse than an eternity of starved terror in a flyblown ditch.

Or maybe I'd fallen asleep and dreamed it. Maybe I was awake now, and if I got up and walked out of the woods, I'd find myself in 2016, never having left. More than once I almost tried. My clothes stopped me. They were not 2016 clothes, so either I was still dreaming or this was no dream.

As day thickened into dusk, I started feeling dizzy and strange. I told myself it was hunger or thirst. But that wasn't it. It was more like a panic attack, or the mother of all panic attacks—a thumping, grinding, heart-squeezing, head-crunching onset of blind, suffocating terror. I was trapped. That was the thing. Trapped in these woods. Trapped on this one stupid small-town block. Trapped in a world that didn't want me, but which wouldn't let me go. A world that might not even be real.

If my world wasn't real, maybe I wasn't real, either. The clothes I wore, and the body in those clothes—the hands before me, their fingernails clumped with dirt—the knuckles of those hands, still scabbed from the beating they'd delivered in the city—

Then was anything real? All the things I remembered might be only a dream. What was it Descartes said? *Cogito ergo* something-or-other: *I think, therefore I am.* But I couldn't think. I couldn't hold on to separate thoughts or follow their logic. So maybe there was no me. Maybe my existence was as fictional as the name John Walker itself.

By then it was dark. Still I remained in the ditch. On a practical level I knew I had to wait until the street was empty of people. On a deeper level I was afraid to move. As long as I gripped the earth—and I did grip it, clutching the damp soil in my fists—and pressed it close to me, I was in contact with something that felt real. Lose that contact, and I might slip away into nothingness.

So I lay there, holding tight to the spinning earth, unsure if I was a person or only some celestial prankster's joke, as the darkness deepened and the night matured.

At ten o'clock I made my move.

X

I KNEW IT was ten by my trusty Fossil watch. I wasn't absolutely certain the street would be deserted at ten—midnight would have been safer—but somehow I knew that if I didn't go now, I would never go at all. I would simply lie in the gully until someone stumbled across me, a half-dead thing in soiled rags.

It took the greatest effort of my life to release my grip on the earth and rise to my feet. I stood there shaking, my knees weak. My throat felt raw, as if I'd been shouting. I remembered a science-fiction story I'd read as a kid, a story that must have dated to around this time. "I Have No Mouth, and I Must Scream"—that was the title, and it was how I felt.

I climbed out of the gully and walked through the woods. My progress was unsteady. My vision wasn't as clear as it should have been. I felt oddly detached from everything, as if I were watching myself from a few feet away.

The fear was still there, but I'd clamped down on it, holding it in a vise. Maybe nothing was real except my will. That sounded like something one of those German philosophers would have said. Nietzsche or somebody. Come to think of it, hadn't Nietzsche insisted that everything that had happened before would happen again? Eternal return, I thought he called it.

I didn't care. The only return that mattered was my return to my own world. For the first time in my life, I found myself praying—praying to God or the universe to drop the barrier and let me pass.

I could have gone east along the inlet, avoiding the street, but I was afraid the police would be watching the rear of the Stevenson place in case their quarry returned.

And somehow I had to face Miller Avenue one more time. Had to retrace the steps that had brought me here. Maybe if I did everything in reverse, headed back the way I had come, I could trick my gatekeepers into letting me out.

Nobody was on the street. I'd caught a break. There'd been a chance the locals would still be sitting outside, talking over the day's excitement. But no, they'd retreated inside their homes. Scared, probably. A killer had been in their midst. He still might be hanging around. Best to take no chances. The kids hadn't been left outside to play, and for once no one lingered on a porch.

A long stretch of empty asphalt extended before me, bracketed by a double row of houses nestled behind honey locust trees and curbside autos. A breeze blew off the ocean, cooling my face. It felt real, even if nothing else did.

I started walking up the street. I was utterly alone, more alone than I'd ever been.

The air was humid and close, the dark corners of the street alive with fireflies. Moths batted against the streetlamps. I saw the flicker of TV sets through windows—people watching *Ironside* or *Mission: Impossible* or whatever was on at this hour. People who would cast their votes for Nixon or McGovern this fall. Well, mostly for Nixon.

A car turned off First Avenue, coming down the street. I made out a rectangular shape on the roof. Wrong season for a ski rack. It was a cop car's dome light.

I took cover behind a tree. This time I definitely uttered the f-word. Another minute, and I might have been out of here. But the man behind the curtain, the great and powerful Oz, just didn't want to make it easy.

The squad car slowed as the officer riding shotgun

directed his flashlight into the bushes skirting Clara and Enid's porch. Something was rustling around in there.

The tree wouldn't conceal me for long. I dropped to all fours and bellied my way to the side of the nearest house. Yes, crawling. I didn't even feel any shame about it. I'd crawled before.

As I cowered behind the corner of the house, I heard a cat's squeal, followed by laughter from the prowl car. It must have been Mr. Tibbs in the bushes.

The cops would be moving on now. They had to.

They didn't. The car advanced slowly, the flashlight probing other lawns.

Even positioned where I was, I would be lit up in another few seconds. I retreated, creeping along the side of the house to the backyard, where I nearly stumbled over a child's pool, the inflatable kind that could be filled with a garden hose. I'd had one just like it when I was a kid.

Well, of course I had. This was 114 Miller—my parents' house. Reduced to instinct and reflex, I hadn't even recognized it.

The yard was empty. From inside the house came low music. Elvis Presley, "In the Ghetto."

A car door shut. I heard a voice. "Could swear I saw something."

The patrolmen, leaving their vehicle.

The other one asked a question I didn't hear.

"Back there," his partner said. "Sneaking into the yard, maybe."

In my head, that voiceless scream was back. Because it wasn't *right*. Wasn't *fair*. I'd done what I was supposed to do. I'd played the game. And still my unseen wardens wouldn't let me go. They waved the key to my cell in front of my face, then palmed it when it was almost in my grasp.

Once again two men in uniform were after me, as their counterparts would be after me on another night and another street, forty-four years in the future.

But they wouldn't get me. I was close to Ground Zero, close enough for one last try. I could evade them for a few minutes longer, half a block more.

The lock on the screen door at the rear of our house had never worked properly. My dad was always promising to fix it, but he never had.

I jiggled the handle. The door yielded. The inside door had been left open. No AC, remember? On summer nights you needed cross ventilation.

As I entered, I stole a glance inside the rec room, where the music was playing. A big transistor radio rested on the coffee table next to an open copy of *Jonathan Livingston Seagull*.

Liz was here. Babysitting. It was a Friday, and my folks were out.

I didn't see her, but a seam of light glowed in the crack under the closed door to the half-bath that we'd called a powder room.

Outside, I heard a jingle of duty belts. The cops were entering the backyard.

I couldn't stay where I was, framed in the screen door, and I couldn't hide in the rec room when Liz might emerge at any moment, so I went up the short flight of stairs to the main level. In the kitchen I hunkered down.

The police wouldn't hang around long. The only danger was that they might ask to search the house. If they did, I was screwed. I'd have to run for it—run out through the front door—and hope they didn't shoot me before I reached Ground Zero.

From downstairs came the flush of a toilet. The radio was still playing "In the Ghetto." A humming voice picked up the melody. Liz was out of the powder room, unaware of the cops in the yard. I hoped she wouldn't hear them. I didn't want her asking questions and maybe being inspired to search the house herself.

Another minute passed. The Presley song ended, and

Johnny Nash came on, singing "I Can See Clearly Now." Liz didn't hum along to that one.

I risked a look out the kitchen window. The backyard was empty. The cops had gone.

Thank God.

Now all I had to do was get out. The front door was the best way. I would wait by the door until I was certain the patrol car had left the area, then make my exit. No need to risk passing by Liz on the ground floor again.

I took my first step out of the kitchen, toward the living room. Behind me, there was a sharp intake of breath, the kind of choked gasp that movie actors never quite get right.

I knew who it was even before I turned. Liz had come up the stairs, the book in her hand. Her feet were bare—that was why I'd heard no steps. Funny how I registered that detail.

She stared at me. Her eyes blinked once. I knew she'd heard everything about the police investigation and their interest in the man calling himself John Walker. And I knew she was seeing my damp, dirt-streaked clothes, my sunburnt face, my tangled hair and frightened eyes.

And I knew she would scream.

In this neighborhood, a scream would cut through the quiet like a siren. And the police couldn't have gone far. They might still be parked outside.

So she couldn't scream. This was the conclusion I reached. I didn't put it into words. I felt it in the sudden itch of my palms, the red rage boiling up out of my fear.

Rage—because I was so close, nearly home, within steps of the portal that simply *had* to be open to me now—and then *she* had to blunder into my path, this aging suburban hippie with her dazed cow eyes and open mouth, this silly caricature of Goldie Hawn grooviness in her striped pantsuit and her pile of bouffant hair, this kitschy mascara'd apparition out of the dead past.

She'd fucked it all up, the stupid *bitch*.

I reached her in one stride, and I hit her, a bare-knuckle slap across the face that sent her tumbling halfway down the stairs, and I was on top of her, my fists rising and falling, blood spritzing the stairway walls. With every blow the back of her head thumped against the steps, but her eyes stayed open, and I knew she was still conscious, still seeing me—seeing me without illusion, seeing me finally for what I was.

"I can see clearly now ..." the radio crooned.

I went on pounding until I knew her eyes would never see anything again.

It looked like she wouldn't remarry, after all, or have children, or vote for McGovern, or even finish reading *Jonathan Livingston Seagull*.

I raised my hands from her body. Once again the knuckles were skinned raw, the fingers bloodied. But my palms weren't itching any longer, and the blaze of rage was already ebbing, the embers safely banked.

Later I might feel remorse. At the moment I felt only an empty exhaustion I knew too well. I was spent, hollowed out, and somehow I almost wasn't surprised when I lifted my head and saw him watching me.

He'd heard the noise and come creeping down the staircase from his bedroom on the top floor. He stood in the kitchen doorway, in his blue pajama shorts. His chest was bare and bony; I'd forgotten how skinny I was at that age.

His gaze met mine, and with a sudden shift of perspective I saw through his eyes. Saw the man with wild hair who knelt on the back stairs, and the bloodstains on the walls, and Mrs. McCall in a boneless heap with her face half-erased.

I saw it, and it was like a knife blade of memory punching through a wall of resistance—an image I'd carried with me for forty-four years, buried so deeply that I couldn't get to it, couldn't remember.

THE STREET

I remembered now. I remembered the night that had changed me, the trauma that had warped my life. It never had anything to do with Mr. Wilson. It was always that other man, the one who'd stopped to talk to me about hot dogs on the boardwalk and comic books and perfect summer days. The crazy man with the red fists and the empty, staring, haunted eyes.

We looked at each other, and there was something timeless in our face-to-face encounter, something like a pause when the world held its breath, and I knew this was it, this moment—this was the pivot point of my life, the fulcrum on which everything turned.

It all began here, ended here. In this place. In this time.

"Don't be afraid," I whispered in a hoarse, hopeless voice.

The pause broke, the universe exhaled, and my ten-year-old self spun on his heel and ran flying toward the front door, and he was screaming, the first long scream in a lifetime of bad dreams, angry outbursts, violent rages, bruised and battered hands.

"Murderer! It's a murderer! It's a murderer!"

It, he said. Not *he*. As if the man on the stairs was not even human.

His cries would rouse the whole neighborhood. Everyone would be after me. They would form a mob and chase me down. Maybe they would beat me to death right there on the street, just as I'd beaten Liz. Bring things full circle ...

But things already had come full circle, hadn't they? A twist in time had folded my life into a Möbius strip. My end was all tangled up in my beginning, and the man was the father of the child he had been.

There could no redemption, not for me.

And Miller Avenue always would be a dead-end street.

I was on my feet. I had to run.

That was my only impulse, simple flight, with no

thought of Ground Zero or anything else. Just a kick of my heart restarting and a surge of panic as I stumbled down the steps, booting *Jonathan Livingston Seagull* out of my way. I'd always hated that stupid book.

I took the back door, cutting across other backyards, heading east without purpose or destination. Already I heard doors slamming, voices carrying in the night, the bloop of the prowl car's siren. And the boy's cries, echoing along the street as they would echo down four decades: *"It's a murderer...!"*

I didn't know how long that boy would keep yelling those words, and mumbling them, and hearing them in his sleep. I only knew that one day he would awake and the words would be gone, along with any recollection of what had happened. And no one would ever speak of it to him again.

I was blundering through a thorny tangle of rosebushes in the sisters' yard when Enid appeared at an upstairs window.

"I see you! I see you, John Walker!"

Goddamn dyke.

I veered along the side of their house, onto the front lawn. Behind me, tires squealed. The squad car swung in a U-turn, bouncing up on the curb. Its high beams spotlighted me like an actor on a stage.

Someone shouted an order to stop. I thought a gunshot would be next. But no one fired. The high beams just kept on brightening as the car accelerated. It would be on top of me in another second.

I could never outrun them. There was nowhere to hide. I was fully exposed in the headlights, with the police at my back and the whole neighborhood turning out in force.

The car slammed to a stop behind me. Shadows fluttered on the pavement—the two cops on foot now, closing in. As I reached the intersection, I cut north, down First Avenue, in the mad hope that I could lose them, which was impossible, because they were right behind me, right at my heels—

Except they weren't.

There was no one on my heels.

And I wasn't on First Avenue. I was on a street in the city, on an autumn night.

Back. I'd come back.

I'd passed through the barrier without even thinking about it. Maybe not thinking was the key. I hadn't been thinking when I'd crossed over the first time. Maybe the trick was to run all out, driven by adrenaline, with no higher consciousness, no awareness except of blood and breath and fear.

Maybe not. I couldn't say. I only knew I'd gotten through. I'd left 1972 behind.

I was home.

I staggered to a stop, leaning on the stoop of a brownstone, fighting to catch my breath.

At first there was no way to tell how much time had passed in the city—a day or a year or no time at all. Then I heard the blare of the siren blocks away, and from up the street, fast footfalls. I lifted my head as two police officers rounded the corner.

Not the ones from Miller Avenue. These were 2016 cops, the pair I'd been outrunning three days ago—but only a few seconds earlier, in this reality, where it seemed I'd hardly been missed.

I half shut my eyes in resignation. It appeared I was fated to be arrested in one era or another. I preferred this one. For one thing, the woman in the bar might live. Liz McCall hadn't.

I was prepared to submit to them. I even started to hold out my hands for the cuffs.

But the first cop hardly glanced at me. "Not him," he yelled to his partner, and he brushed past the stoop, the second man following, as they charged ahead into the dark.

Not him?

I thought of my face, grizzled with a new beard, burned by the sun, scored by mosquito bites. My clothes, ridiculously out-of-date thrift-shop apparel. The dirt all over me. The cloud of body odor. The matted pile of my hair ...

I wasn't the man in an overcoat who'd eluded them only seconds earlier. That man had been neatly groomed and properly attired, a middle-class bar patron, not a homeless derelict.

If they'd seen Liz's blood on my hands, they would have hesitated. But they'd been in a hurry, and the street was dark.

So I was off the hook. I'd gotten away with it—first in 1972, and now here.

And ... next time? Who could say?

But there would be a next time. That much I knew.

I would never be a normal man. Never be free of the demons that possessed me. I had written my fate in the very act of trying to erase it. I had made my own hell, and I must live it, and nothing would change for me, ever. And time doubles back on itself as the snake swallows its tail in the closed circle of my life.

I was cold without a coat, but I didn't mind. I had my wallet. I could find a taxi stand and get a ride home.

With my head down and my hands in my pockets, I started moving. Somewhere on a parallel street, the siren wailed, a long, shuddering cry like a child's scream. As I walked away into the night, I heard that scream rising around me and within me.

I will hear it always.

p.s.

The author walks his dog near Trouble Pond in the late 1960s.

Acknowledgments

THIS SHORT NOVEL was a departure from my usual thrillers. I had some fun with it, and I hope you did, too.

Please visit me at www.michaelprescott.net, where you'll find links to all my books, news about upcoming projects, contact info, and other good stuff.

As always, special thanks to Diana Cox of www.novelproofreading.com for another meticulous proof-reading job. I did some additional rewriting after she reviewed the manuscript, so if there any mistakes, they're my own.

—MP

ABOUT THE AUTHOR

AFTER TWENTY YEARS in traditional publishing, Michael Prescott found himself unable to sell another book. On a whim, he began releasing his novels in digital form. Sales took off, and by 2011 he was one of the world's best-selling e-book writers.